"You think you've got everyone's darkest secrets figured out, while you're Little Miss Perfect," Devon shouted. "Well, you have no right to be so sanctimonious! You're the one who was cheating on me!"

Elizabeth felt the color drain from her face. A tiny part of her brain, the part that was still rational, was shocked to realize she actually wanted to strike him. That she was actually going to strike him. She raised a hand to slap him across his strong, angular jaw. . . .

But something hit her first. It slammed into her feet from below, throwing her off balance and jamming every joint in her body. Devon grabbed her arm, the anger in his face transformed to fear. Impossibly, the water in the pool reached up as a single entity, like a sea serpent coming to life, before sloshing back into its container, roiling frenetically. The patio around the pool rippled like water. Deep below the earth's surface a power like nothing Elizabeth had ever imagined rumbled and roared and threatened to tear her world apart. The music went dead.

Then a girl's voice screamed, "Earthquake!"

Visit the Official Sweet Valley Web Site on the Internet at:

http://www.sweetvalley.com

LAST
WISH

Written by
Kate William

Created by
FRANCINE PASCAL

BANTAM BOOKS
NEW YORK • TORONTO • LONDON • SYDNEY • AUCKLAND

RL 6, age 12 and up

LAST WISH

A Bantam Book / September 1998

Sweet Valley High® is a registered trademark of Francine Pascal.
Conceived by Francine Pascal.
Produced by 17th Street Productions, a division of Daniel Weiss Associates, Inc.
33 West 17th Street
New York, NY 10011.
Cover photography by Michael Segal.

ISBN: 0-553-49235-7

Published simultaneously in the United States and Canada

Bantam Books are published by Bantam Books, a division of Bantam
Doubleday Dell Publishing Group, Inc. Its trademark, consisting of the
words "Bantam Books" and the portrayal of a rooster, is Registered in U.S.
Patent and Trademark Office and in other countries. Marca Registrada.
Bantam Books, 1540 Broadway, New York, New York 10036.

PRINTED IN THE UNITED STATES OF AMERICA

OPM   0 9 8 7 6 5 4 3

To Mia Pascal Johansson

Chapter 1

Elizabeth Wakefield stared out her window at the sparkling surface of her family's swimming pool. Her lips pursed in thought as she twirled a strand of golden hair between her fingers. Suddenly she spun to face her friends. "I know! We can have a costume party—one with a theme!"

Enid Rollins nodded, her reddish brown hair bobbing against her shoulders. "That's not bad," she said. "We could tell everyone to come as a literary character." She jumped up from Elizabeth's desk chair and curtsied, holding out an imaginary full skirt over her khaki walking shorts. "I can be Jane Eyre!"

Maria Slater rolled her deep brown eyes. "And Jessica and Lila will be Tweedledee and Tweedledum. As if!"

Elizabeth giggled. "Oops. I guess you're right. I keep forgetting this isn't *my* seventeenth birthday party we're planning—it's my twin's."

"But it's your birthday too!" Olivia Davidson said, perched at the foot of Elizabeth's bed with the California sunshine gilding her mane of wild brown curls like a halo. "Why shouldn't you do something you think is fun?"

"Hello!" Maria broke in, a wry expression on her ebony face. "Remember, Jessica's favorite literary character is the woman who gives makeup tips in *Ingenue* magazine."

"There has to be something we can do that will be fun for *everyone*," Elizabeth said, her hands in the pockets of her jeans.

"True," said Enid. "This isn't just a birthday party. It'll also be an end-of-the-school-year blowout."

"Still, I want to surprise Jessica with a party planned especially for her," Elizabeth said. "But it's not easy, coming up with a party both our sets of friends will like!"

Elizabeth and Jessica had the same sun blond hair, blue-green eyes, heart-shaped faces, and size-six figures. But the resemblance was purely physical. When it came to personality and interests, the twins were nothing alike.

Impulsive, irrepressible Jessica spent as little time

on schoolwork as possible, convinced there were more important things in life—like cheerleading, shopping, and scoping for guys on the beach. Elizabeth, four minutes older, was the more responsible twin, a straight-A student who worked hard on the school newspaper, the *Oracle*, and dreamed of becoming a professional writer. Jessica was happy to date somebody new each week, while Elizabeth preferred a steady relationship with one special boy.

One special boy. Elizabeth bit her lip at the thought. Until recently that boy had been Todd Wilkins, the Sweet Valley High basketball star she'd been dating for what Jessica thought was an eternity. Elizabeth had been deeply in love with Todd. In a way she supposed she still was—though they were barely speaking to each other now. Elizabeth knew she'd hurt Todd terribly when she fell for Devon Whitelaw, the new guy at school. But she couldn't ignore her attraction to tall, handsome Devon, with his independent attitude and razor-sharp mind. Her confusion had cost her both boyfriends. She and Devon were officially "just friends" now, and she figured she should feel lucky for that. At least Devon didn't hate her, though he had every right to.

Olivia's voice broke into her thoughts. "Well, today is Sunday, the first of June," Olivia was

3

saying. "Your birthday is the thirteenth."

"That's less than two weeks to plan the birthday bash of the century, whatever you decide to do for it," Maria added.

"Don't remind me," Elizabeth said with a groan. She shoved away all thoughts of Todd and Devon and tried to concentrate on the issue at hand.

Elizabeth's gaze rested on Olivia's color-splashed tunic and purple leggings. "Come on, Liv. You're the most creative person in our class. You must have some ideas!"

"Give me time!" Olivia chided. "The *Mona Lisa* wasn't painted overnight!"

"Speaking of ideas, Liz, have you picked out a birthday present for Jessica?" Maria asked.

Elizabeth shook her head. "The party will be part of it—if I ever get it planned. I do want to give her something else, but I haven't a clue about what!"

"Choosing a gift couldn't be too hard, knowing Jessica," Maria pointed out, reaching out to scratch Prince Albert, the Wakefields' golden retriever, behind the ears. "She's always so in-your-face about telling the world what she wants."

"True," Enid said. "But Chris O'Donnell is already married."

Elizabeth laughed. "With Chris out of the picture, Jess's second choice would be a new car since our

4

Jeep bit the big one. But my savings account isn't up to the challenge."

"Olivia, how are you coming on your gift for Ken?" Maria asked.

Elizabeth looked up, interested. Olivia had been dating Elizabeth's friend Ken Matthews, quarterback for Sweet Valley High's football team, and Elizabeth had never seen either of them looking so happy. "What gift?" she asked. "Are you planning something special for the end of the school year?"

"I'm painting his portrait!" Olivia revealed, her hazel eyes sparkling. "I'm just about finished, and I can't wait to see if he likes it."

"You mean he hasn't seen it yet?" Enid asked. "Didn't he have to pose for you?"

"Nope. I asked him for photographs for reference. Besides that I'm making it up out of my head."

"You go, girl!" Maria cheered. "Hey, Liz, how about surprising Jessica with a painting party for your mutual birthday? Everyone can wear old clothes—"

"Painter's pants?" Enid quipped.

"We can tape up a mural-size sheet of paper on the side of the house," Maria continued. "And everyone can paint their greetings to Jessica on it. I went to a party like that once in Hollywood. Everyone threw paint all over each other. It was total insanity, but we never stopped laughing."

Olivia grinned. "It sounds like fun, but isn't Jessica more the dressed-to-the-hilt type when it comes to parties?"

Elizabeth nodded. "I'm sure Jessica's life on the planet would end if a guy saw her with a blob of paint in her hair."

"It's a good thing Ken doesn't feel that way!" Olivia said, rubbing at some multicolored smears of dried paint on her own hands. "When I'm working, my hair gets so much paint in it, you'd think I'd gotten a punked-out dye job!"

"And on you, Liv, it looks perfect," Elizabeth told her warmly. "Very painterly."

Olivia smiled back.

"But we're still stuck for an idea for the hottest birthday party ever," Enid reminded them.

Maria ran a hand over her stylishly short black hair. "That's because we're going about this all wrong," she said. "We have to start thinking like Jessica."

Olivia grimaced. "That sounds painful!"

"It does, but Maria's right," Elizabeth said. "What kind of party would Jessica want?"

"Something with blasting music," Maria said.

"And hot guys," Enid said.

"She'd want to have it at a place where she can wear the sexiest minidress Valley Mall has to offer," Olivia added.

"I've got it!" Elizabeth cried. She raced to the bed and plopped down in the middle of it, disheveling the comforter. "We'll rent the entire Beach Disco!" she exclaimed. "Hire a DJ or a band and invite everyone we know!"

"And dance the night away!" Maria finished for her.

Enid nodded. "That's perfect! Jessica loves that place."

"So does everyone else," Olivia said. "Dancing in the open air, with a view of the ocean . . . Hey, Ken and I are definitely there."

"I've never heard of anyone renting the whole disco," Enid pointed out. "Are you sure you can afford it?"

"I don't know what it would cost," Elizabeth admitted. "But it can't be too outrageous. And maybe they'll give us a discount because we hang out there all the time."

"A frequent dancer credit," Maria joked.

"Right." Elizabeth swatted her friend on the arm. "Whatever it costs, it'll be worth it. We've only got one birthday a year, right?"

"And you only turn seventeen once," Olivia said.

Elizabeth took a deep breath. "I can hardly believe we're going to be seventeen years old!" she exclaimed. "I'm sure this will be a birthday we'll remember forever."

7

"Come on, you two," Jessica urged, dipping a toe into Lila's enormous backyard swimming pool. "We've got to come up with the world's coolest party idea!"

Lila looked up from the inflatable raft she was floating on, her back shining with suntan oil above the band of her orange bikini briefs. "I still say we should auction off all the guys as dates. But you said it wouldn't be Liz's thing."

Amy Sutton pulled herself out of the water and sat on the edge of the pool beside Jessica. "Well, it *ought* to be Liz's thing," Amy said, adjusting the straps of her black one-piece suit. "It's not like she's an item with anyone."

"I keep suggesting guys she could go out with," Jessica said. "But you know Liz. She's more worried about them having brains than anything important, like their cars or their bods."

"I can't believe your sister threw away two of the best-looking guys in the whole class!" Amy complained. "Has she even had a single date since she decided Todd and Devon weren't good enough for her?"

"Who cares?" Lila asked. "If the twerp twin is off the dating track, that just leaves more guys for us. Well, for me and Jessica anyway, Amy—since you're still joined at the hip with Barry Rork."

Amy jerked her foot through the water, sending a glittering arc splashing over Lila's legs. "You're just jealous because I have a steady boyfriend."

"Jealous of you and Barry?" Lila asked, her right eyebrow arching past the top rim of her designer sunglasses. *"Puh-lease."*

"What's wrong with—"

Jessica held up a hand. "Get over yourselves, girl-friends. We've got a major party to plan. Can you believe I'm going to be seventeen years old? Finally!"

"Well, you can't turn seventeen without a really radical party," Amy said. "If we can think one up."

"So what's wrong with auctioning off the guys?" Lila demanded.

"Liz would hate it!" Jessica said. "And besides, you're the only one around who could afford one!"

Lila lifted her sunglasses to stare down her nose at her friends. "Explain the part where this is bad."

Amy's waist-length hair, usually white blond, was soaked to a near brown. She pulled it to one side and twisted it in her hands to wring out the water. "OK, then how about a rock concert? Rhomboid is playing in Los Angeles that weekend. We can do a road trip."

"That would be so awesome!" Jessica said, but then sighed. "But not for Liz. She thinks Rhomboid sounds like a wrecking ball demolishing a skyscraper full of sick cats."

9

"Your twin is so uncool," Amy complained.

"Don't remind me," Jessica said.

"So let's blow off your lesser half and just celebrate *your* birthday," Lila suggested.

Jessica shook her head. "I can't do that. Liz may be as dull as algebra, but she's still my sister, and I owe her."

"Because she's helping you pass French?" Amy asked.

"Because she lets you borrow the few clothes she's got that are worth borrowing?" Lila asked.

"No, because she's been bailing me out of trouble all year! I want to make her seventeenth birthday— *our* seventeenth birthday—something special. We have to come up with a party Liz and her brainiac friends will like."

"Here's the plan!" Lila exclaimed. "We rent a video for Elizabeth and the other dweebs down in Dullsville, pop them up a bowl of popcorn, and leave them in nerd heaven in front of the television—"

"—while *we* go to L.A. to see Rhomboid!" Amy finished gleefully.

"Ha, ha," Jessica countered. "You two are no help at all. The problem is, we've got to think like Elizabeth. We've got to think *dull!*"

"A poetry reading?" Amy suggested, wincing.

Lila nodded, then leaned back, tilting her face

toward the sun. "Definitely yawn worthy. That's the spirit."

"But it's not much of a celebration," Jessica said.

"Isn't there some kind of party that would be boring enough to satisfy Liz without putting the rest of us into a coma?" Amy asked.

Jessica glanced around at the terraced gardens, Olympic-size pool, and Mediterranean-style bathhouse of Fowler Crest. As always, she couldn't help reflecting on how grand the grounds of Lila's home seemed compared to her own pleasant but simple backyard. "Elizabeth likes things simple. What can we do that's simple? How about a backyard picnic at my house?"

Lila shuddered visibly. "With hamburgers and stuff? That's certainly an improvement over my idea. Juvenile, yet unoriginal."

"Right, and we can go *bowling* afterward," Amy said, rolling her smoke gray eyes. "I can already feel the coolness draining from my body."

Jessica sighed. "Face it, when it comes to being bland, we totally suck."

Lila sat up suddenly, nearly overturning the inflatable raft. "Wait a minute. We're doing this all wrong!" she told them after she'd regained her balance. "What about if we replace the word *dullness* with the word *elegance*?"

Jessica nodded thoughtfully, anticipation rising in

her chest. She could see her best friend's brain working, clicking into its famous party-planning mode. "I'm with you so far," Jessica said. "Elizabeth may be boring, but she's a sucker for elegance. What do you have in mind?"

"A jazz quartet," Lila said slowly. "Under one of those big rented tents. With dancing. And a table full of catered hors d'oeuvres . . ."

"Where?" Jessica asked.

"Bruce Patman's beach house?" Amy suggested. "You've got to admit, the last party there was totally kicking."

"I'd like to totally kick Bruce!" Jessica said. "I don't care if he is rich and good-looking. He's too obnoxious a person to deserve a ritzy beach house."

"So where else could we do it?" Amy asked.

Jessica shrugged. "What about right here at Fowler Crest?"

"Noooo, I don't think so," Lila replied, shaking her head. "After holding the preprom party *and* the postprom brunch here, my parents have put me on party probation. Besides, for Liz it's got to be a simpler setting, like you said. Something less formal. All this beauty and sophistication would be wasted on her and her geek friends."

Jessica glanced around at the brilliantly sunlit afternoon. Suddenly the perfect idea came to her.

"We don't need a mansion or a beach house!" she squealed. "Let's just do it with a tent on the beach! Elizabeth loves the ocean."

"Yes!" Lila agreed. "That is so totally perfect!"

A cloud drifted over the sun. "Wait a sec," Jessica said, tapping herself on the cheek. "Get a clue, Wakefield. We're talking about *my* budget. I could probably swing a tent rental. Maybe even food if I bum some cash off my brother. But a jazz quartet?"

Amy grimaced. "Yeah. The bank of Steven Wakefield probably couldn't cover that."

Lila waved a hand. "Don't worry about it. My father has this software designer at his firm who's also a cellist. She's in a fabulous quartet that plays at all the company functions."

"If they're that fabulous, they're priced way out of my league," Jessica said.

"Naturally," Lila agreed smugly. "But if the boss's daughter referred you, she'll cut you a deal."

"Music, schmusic," Amy said. "We haven't even begun to consider the most crucial thing of all."

"What's that?" Jessica asked.

Amy rolled her eyes. "Hello? Our outfits, of course."

Chapter 2

Todd Wilkins groaned as his ball ricocheted off the rim of the basket and bounced away along the circular driveway of the Wilkinses' house. "Sunday afternoons reek," he complained.

Aaron Dallas chased the ball, scooped it up expertly, and hooked it through the hoop. Todd reached in halfheartedly to make the catch, but Aaron grabbed the ball first and held it against his chest, stopping the game. "You never used to hate Sunday afternoons," Aaron reminded him. "And you never used to miss easy baskets like that one. What's bugging you, man?"

"Nothing," Todd insisted, glaring down at his friend from his own six-foot-three vantage point. "Let's shut up and play. I thought this was a basketball game."

Aaron rolled his eyes. "This isn't a game; it's a massacre. You're the hotshot hoops star, but I'm totally kicking your butt."

"So I'm having a sucky day," Todd said with a shrug.

"It's a heckuva lot more than a sucky day when a soccer hack can beat Whizzer Wilkins at his own game. What's stressing you, man?"

"Nimrods who want to gab instead of shooting hoops."

Aaron shook his head knowingly. "It's Elizabeth, isn't it?"

"No way!" Todd objected. At the sound of Elizabeth's name he felt a knife turn in his gut. At the same time his fists clenched in anger over how she'd treated him. "I am so over her."

Aaron stared at him expectantly, absently bouncing the ball from hand to hand in front of him. "Right. You're not freaking over Liz. Now tell me about Santa Claus and the tooth fairy."

Todd ran his fingers through his curly brown hair. He sighed heavily and sat in the grass along the edge of the driveway. "OK, so it's Liz. Isn't it always Liz?"

"Have you talked to her?" Aaron asked.

"Talk to her? I go totally zomboid every time I pass her in the hallway at school," Todd admitted.

"I guess I figured the two of you would get back together," Aaron said, settling himself onto the grass beside Todd, "now that she and Whitelaw are just friends."

"Devon Whitelaw!" Todd spat out the name. "What a loser." He took a deep breath and shook his head. "But to be honest, I can't believe he'd even want to be friends with her after what she pulled at the prom. She used us both."

"It's hard to believe," Aaron said. "I mean, you and Liz were a thing for so long. Of all the couples at school, you were the ones I figured would, you know . . ." Aaron's voice trailed off and he looked away.

"So did I," Todd said. "But not anymore. After what she did to me—" Todd scowled. "I'll tell you one thing, Whitelaw must be one forgiving guy."

He still couldn't believe Elizabeth had danced with him at the prom while she knew that across the room, Devon was dancing with Jessica and thinking *he* was with Elizabeth. Todd had never thought of Elizabeth as the deceitful twin. Jessica was the one who'd go to elaborate lengths to date two guys at once, even if it meant humiliating them both in front of everyone. Now he wondered if he'd ever really known Elizabeth at all.

Aaron practiced spinning the basketball balanced on one finger. "At least school's almost out," he said. "Only two more weeks of classes and then exams.

After that you won't have to see her every day."

"Yeah, right," Todd scoffed. "It isn't that big a town. I'll probably run into her all over the place. The beach, the movies, the Dairi Burger . . ."

Aaron lay back on the grass and tossed the basketball straight up, squinting at the sky so he could see to catch it. "Maybe you should get away for a while," he suggested. "Leave Sweet Valley for the summer. The farther, the better."

Todd stared at his family's brick-fronted home. "Right. Like the parental units are going to let me spend the next two months backpacking across Tibet."

"They might let you visit your friends in Vermont, or spend the summer with relatives, or apply to one of those sports camps that colleges organize."

Todd shrugged. "I don't know."

"Well, I do," Aaron said, sitting up suddenly and tossing him the ball. "What good will it do to hang around here all summer, being more and more miserable? Believe me, if your mood gets any worse, it'll be the rest of us who are trying to get away."

Todd rose slowly without speaking and began dribbling the ball on the pavement. He aimed carefully, and the ball smacked against the backboard before dropping through the basket.

"I'll think about it," he said finally. Maybe, he thought, getting away wasn't such a bad idea.

Out of sight, out of mind and all that.

Aaron shrugged. "I'd say the ball's in your court."

Ken Matthews lounged against a leather-paneled wall in the Patman family rec room and watched Bruce Patman pull his monogrammed pool cue from the stand. The engraved brass plaque on the handle read 1BRUCE1, the same as the custom license plates on Bruce's black Porsche. Ken rolled his eyes.

For a moment he wondered what had possessed him to spend his Sunday afternoon playing pool with Bruce, of all people. But he knew exactly why he was there. Winston Egbert had talked him into coming along. "If it's just me and Bruce, he'll win every single game," Winston had complained on the phone. "You wouldn't want Bruce's head to swell up any bigger, would you? We'd have to float him over football games."

As usual, Winston could talk him into almost anything. So now the two juniors stood watching as tall, arrogant Bruce made a big show of chalking his cue. Ken had always considered himself a decent pool player. He'd been sure he could whip Bruce, even if the guy did live in a mansion with a luxurious, well-equipped basement room devoted entirely to pool and billiards. Now he watched as Bruce expertly sank four balls on the break. *I don't stand a chance of beating him,* he suddenly realized, *at least not on Patman turf.*

Luckily, Ken decided, he had more interesting things to think about than Bruce's pool game. "Olivia's almost finished with the portrait she's painting of me," he confided to Winston.

"That is so cool," Winston said. "Maybe she'll paint me next." Always the class clown, Winston bent his tall, skinny frame, posing with his chin on the back of one hand and his elbow on his knee. "She could paint me as *Winston the Thinker.*" He placed one hand to his brow and peered out melodramatically, then pantomimed rowing. "How about *Winston Crossing the Delaware?*"

"How about *Winston Crossing His Eyes?*" Bruce asked. "It would be a lot closer to capturing your true personality—or lack thereof." He pushed a lock of straight dark brown hair out of his eyes and scrutinized the arrangement of balls on the table. "Seven in the corner pocket," he announced before calmly shooting it in.

"You're lucky to have a girlfriend who can paint," Winston said to Ken. He buffed his fingernails on his T-shirt. "Of course, Maria Santelli adores me. But she's not an artist. On the other hand, she *is* a cheerleader. Maybe she'll write a cheer about me."

Ken laughed. "But you don't play any sports."

"Certainly not pool," Bruce added with a snicker. "Three ball in the side pocket."

Winston lowered his eyebrows comically, and the ball rolled exactly where Bruce intended. "I don't know why we thought we could compete with this guy," he said. "After all, he's practically a high-school graduate and we're mere juniors—or should I say, *rising seniors?*"

Ken laughed. "Just be grateful we're not playing for money."

Bruce only smirked.

"Playing? That implies actually getting a chance to strike a ball," Winston reminded Ken. "I won't hold my breath. So, let's talk about something less depressing. What's your portrait look like, Ken?"

"I don't know yet," Ken admitted. "Olivia doesn't want me to see it until it's finished."

Winston grinned. "Those sensitive, temperamental artsy types."

"It's flattering, being painted by an artist as talented as Olivia," Ken admitted, imagining what it would feel like to see his own familiar blond hair and deep-set blue eyes translated to canvas and paint. "Wouldn't that be something if she's a famous artist someday? My portrait could be hanging in a museum!"

Bruce looked up from the pool table. "What is this, Matthews?" he asked, his voice laced with disgust. "Your campaign for Self-centered Weenie of the Year?"

Winston grinned mischievously. "As defending champion, Bruce, are you nervous?"

"You should leave your brain to science, Egbert," Bruce advised. "Science *fiction*."

"Of course, having your picture in a museum is nothing compared to Bruce's exciting life," Winston said. He faked an atrocious New England accent. "After all, His Lordship is attending Harvard University next year. We're lucky he's willing to be seen with riffraff like us."

Ken noticed a pained expression creep over Bruce's features. "I'm not so sure Bruce *is* willing to be seen with us." Ken shook his head. "Notice he's got us in the basement instead of out in public where the rest of the Ivy League might catch him fraternizing with the lower classes."

"Frankly, I was surprised that Harvard let Bruce in," Winston confided. "Did you hear about his test scores?"

Bruce's pale blue eyes flashed cold fire.

"—I heard he scored in the negative numbers on the humility section of the SAT," Winston concluded.

Bruce studied the pool table coolly, but he was clenching his cue so tightly that his fingers were as white as ice. Ken willed Winston to keep his mouth shut. If he pushed Bruce any further, he could find himself impaled by a very expensive pool cue.

"You're just jealous that I'll be hanging out with the rich and famous at the most respected university in the country while you're both stuck here in this backwoods town," Bruce said finally. It was true to Patman's usual snooty banter, but Ken thought his voice sounded harsh, even for Bruce. "Six ball in the side."

"No way, dude!" Winston protested as Bruce leaned over to sight along the edge of his cue stick. "You'd have to be an octopus to make that shot."

Bruce glanced at him out of the corner of his eye and shifted position so that he was holding the cue behind his back. He hammered the cue ball, and it slammed into the eight, which bounced off the rim and knocked against the six ball, which shot across the table, ricocheted off the corner, and rolled neatly into the side pocket.

Ken was impressed despite himself. "Show-off!"

"Face it, plebes. You're toast," Bruce replied. Again his voice held a razor-sharp edge. Instead of its customary smug smile, Bruce's mouth was set in a hard, determined line. Ken had always thought of Bruce as overly competitive. But for a guy who was cleaning the table with them both, his manner was downright grim.

Chapter 3

Jessica breezed into the bathroom that connected the twins' rooms and shut the door behind her to keep the dog from following.

"OK, are you *ever* going to learn to knock?" Elizabeth demanded, looking in the mirror as she clipped a barrette into her hair.

"Excuse me for breathing. When are *you* going to learn that knocking is not my style?" Jessica returned. "And good morning to you too."

"Sorry," Elizabeth said. "Good morning. But as I remember, you already spent at least an hour in here. Isn't it my turn now?"

Jessica shrugged, comparing her own reflection with her sister's. Jessica's hair was arranged in loose, sexy waves that framed her face and called attention to her lilac eye shadow and perfectly applied lipstick. Elizabeth, as usual, wore no styling gel and little makeup. "What for?" Jessica asked. "It's not like you *do* anything with yourself."

"Thanks a lot."

"Besides, I have an important question to ask you," Jessica said.

"No, I'm not telling what I'm getting you for our birthday!" Elizabeth exclaimed with an amused twinkle in her eyes.

Jessica cocked an eyebrow. How did Elizabeth always know what she was thinking? She hated being predictable. But Elizabeth almost always managed to save some of her allowance. Jessica was counting on her for a cool gift. "That wasn't my question," Jessica lied. "I wanted to know, um, do you think my skirt is too long?"

Elizabeth glanced down at Jessica's lime green miniskirt. "Too long?" she asked with a laugh. "Only if it's trying to be a bikini."

Jessica inspected her sister's loose batik pants and mauve T-shirt. "You know, Liz, you could borrow something of mine if you want to be a little more fashion forward."

Elizabeth put her hands on her hips. "What's wrong with what I'm wearing?"

"Nothing, I guess," Jessica said. "I suppose it's

kind of, uh . . . *cute,* in an Olivia Davidson, hippie-artist sort of way."

"What's that supposed to mean?" Elizabeth demanded.

"Don't lose your water. I didn't mean to diss your weirdo friend. But now that you're a free agent, you might want to go for a sexier look."

"A free agent?"

"You know, the post-Todd, post-Devon period. As in playing the field?"

Elizabeth crossed her arms in front of her. "This I've got to hear."

"Take it from me, the best way to get men is to wear something high cut or low cut." Jessica gestured down at her own cropped top.

"What makes you think I want a man?"

"I didn't say *a man.* I said *men.* As in plural," Jessica corrected. "That's been your problem all along—this insane idea that you can date only one at a time."

"Todd and Devon didn't think it was totally fatal," Elizabeth said quietly. "Look what happened when I tried to date both of them. *That* little maneuver killed my love life."

Jessica leaned in toward the mirror and dabbed some lip balm over her lipstick for shine. "Only because you didn't train them properly."

"*Train* them? Are we talking about boyfriends

or dogs?" Elizabeth asked. She grabbed a brush and pulled it vigorously through her hair.

Jessica's finger froze midlip. "There's a difference?"

Elizabeth rolled her eyes.

Jessica decided it was time to change the subject. "You know, there's this darling minidress Lila and I saw in the display window at Lisette's," Jessica began carefully, standing up straight. "It's bright turquoise and cut down to here—perfect for catching a guy's attention. And it looked fantastic on me!" Jessica noticed the corners of her sister's mouth twitching upward and sighed impatiently. "What I mean is, if it looks awesome on me, it'll look awesome on you. You can borrow it if you want after I buy it." She stopped, biting her lip for effect. "Except—"

"Except for what?"

Jessica sighed dramatically. "I just remembered that my savings account is on the critical list. It could be decades before I can afford to buy any new clothes."

"That's too bad," Elizabeth said noncommittally.

"Of course, our birthday is this month," Jessica began, letting a note of hope creep into her voice. "Maybe *somebody* will buy that dress for me. I mean, if anyone was trying to decide what to get me, that dress would be an excellent choice." She glanced hopefully at Elizabeth's reflection in the mirror, but her sister showed no sign of picking up on the hint. For the one who was supposed to be the smart twin, Jessica reflected, Elizabeth could be too dense for words.

"Speaking of our birthday," Elizabeth said, "have you thought about how we should celebrate? Mom's been asking if we want to do a family thing."

Jessica scowled. "With our parents? That would earn us a nomination in the Geek Hall of Fame."

"Well, do you have a better idea?" Elizabeth persisted, studying two different pairs of earrings in an obvious attempt at nonchalance. "I mean, have you thought about throwing ourselves . . . oh, a *party* or something?"

Jessica chuckled inwardly, realizing she was now the one being pumped for information. Throwing a birthday bash wasn't Elizabeth's style. Jessica was the party girl. Elizabeth was obviously dying to know if she was planning a surprise party. *And people say* I'm *the unsubtle one.* "Wrong!"

Elizabeth's hands stopped in the middle of pulling off a gold earring back. "Since when are you against throwing a party?"

"I was talking about the earrings," Jessica announced. She pulled the simple gold studs from

Elizabeth's hand and pointed to the other pair. "The little ones are totally wrong for the outfit. Go with the dangling silver things."

Elizabeth shrugged and picked up the silver earrings. "So what about a birthday party?" she asked again, staring intently at Jessica's reflection as if to gauge her reaction. "Have you thought about having one?"

Jessica laughed. "Oh, you know me—live for the moment and all that. Our birthday isn't until a week from Friday. Thinking that far ahead gives me migraines."

After school that day Bruce whipped his Porsche around the hairpin curves of Valley Crest Drive. The tree-lined road wound up a hill in the wealthiest neighborhood in town, past beautifully landscaped estates. But Bruce barely noticed the scenery blurring by his smoke-tinted windows. Despite the artificially cool breeze from his car's climate control system, he felt warm, almost feverish. He had to get home—now.

He rounded the last bend before the Patman estate. Just ahead a Mercedes was inching out of the driveway of his neighbors' mansion. "I don't have time for this crap!" Bruce leaned on his horn, blaring out a warning. The Mercedes backed off, letting him pass.

Bruce jetted into the Patman driveway, skidded to a halt, and leaped out of the Porsche. Then he raced up the slate walkway and inside through the ornately carved double doors. As usual the day's mail sat on an antique washstand in the foyer, neatly sorted by one of the servants. Bruce's hands were trembling as he grabbed his own pile and rifled through it.

"Come on, Harvard admissions office!" he whispered under his breath. "Dammit, where is that letter?"

Disgusted, he threw down the stack of envelopes and ads, not caring that half of them tumbled to the parquet floor. That's what servants were for. He pawed through his father's mail, his mother's, and his cousin Roger's, praying that his acceptance letter from Harvard had been mistakenly stuck in someone else's pile.

The other Ivy League schools Bruce had applied to had rejected him outright. But his grandfather Reginald Rainer Patman was a Harvard graduate, and so was his great-grandfather William Patman. So he'd assumed he was a shoo-in. In March, when he received the letter turning him down for admission but placing his name on the waiting list, Bruce assumed it was a formality. So what if his grades and SAT scores were a little below par? He was a

Patman, after all. He even had a written recommendation from a former U.S. congressman. They wouldn't dare reject his application—not after he'd told everyone at school that he'd been accepted. Would they?

"Dwight! Miranda!" Bruce yelled. Like magic the two servants appeared in the foyer. "Is this all of today's mail?"

Miranda shrank back from his accusatory tone. "I believe that's everything," she said in a timid voice.

"Is there something else you were expecting?" Dwight asked. "Perhaps tomorrow—"

Without waiting for him to finish, Bruce spun on his heel and stalked upstairs.

Monday afternoon Elizabeth emerged from the blue hatchback Enid shared with her mom and squinted in the dazzling sunshine that reflected off the Pacific Ocean. Elizabeth breathed deeply, feeling the fresh tang of salt water rushing into her lungs.

"This is going to be the most rocking bash in the history of Sweet Valley!" Enid exclaimed, locking the driver's side door. Her voice was dwarfed by the crash of surf on the beach.

Elizabeth smiled gratefully. She knew she was good at planning and organizing things, but a raucous party with loud music and most of the junior class was a little out of her league. She was actually a bit nervous. "I hope I can pull it off," she said, raising her voice to be heard over the pounding waves. "This is more Jessica's style than mine."

"That is the whole idea, isn't it?" Enid asked as they walked across the parking lot.

"I guess so," Elizabeth said, looking up at the Beach Disco. The popular nightspot had a dance floor that began inside and extended through a wall of sliding glass doors onto a large deck overlooking the beach.

"This place is so totally cool at night," Enid said with a laugh. "It's easy to forget how seedy it looks during the day!"

"It *is* kind of falling apart," Elizabeth agreed, nodding toward the weathered gray boards that sided the building. "But you can't beat the setting!" For a moment she thought wistfully of all the times she and Todd had danced together on the open-air deck, under the stars and with a view of the beach. She sighed and shoved the thought away. This was no time to dwell on the past. The twins' seventeenth birthday was approaching, and Elizabeth had a surprise party to plan.

Enid swung open the plate-glass door, and the girls stepped inside. Elizabeth felt instantly stifled.

All the doors to the deck were closed, and the air in the club was thicker than a milk shake.

"Freaky," Enid said. Her voice sounded dull in the murky silence.

"Hello?" Elizabeth called. She cleared her throat. "Is anybody here?"

A loud clatter sounded from the back of the club, followed by an even louder crash. Elizabeth jumped and felt Enid inch closer to her. Finally a short, fat, balding man emerged from a door marked Office and shuffled his way over to the DJ booth. He was wearing a tight white tank top spotted with dampness, and his few wisps of hair were sticking straight up. He rubbed his eyes.

"Help you?" he said in a gruff voice.

Elizabeth squared her shoulders and crossed the room in a few long strides, Enid close behind. "I'm Elizabeth Wakefield," she said, offering her hand.

The man looked at it for a minute, then grasped it quickly. His hand was so sweaty, it felt as if he had just dipped it in a vat of soup. Elizabeth fought the urge to wipe her hand on her skirt.

"Mel," the man said. His beady eyes flicked over Elizabeth, then landed on Enid. He flashed her a toothy grin, and Enid turned red and stared at the floor.

Elizabeth swallowed. "Uh . . . I was wondering

about renting out the club for a birthday party on Friday the thirteenth," she said.

"Can't do it," Mel said, never taking his eyes off Enid.

Elizabeth's heart dropped. "Just like that?" she asked.

"Unless you can guarantee a hundred people will be here and can put down a hefty deposit right now," Mel said, finally looking at Elizabeth.

"A hundred people?" Enid gasped.

Mel grinned again. "And what's your name, little lady?" he asked, looking at Enid.

"Eee . . . Alexandra," Enid said, supplying her middle name.

Quick thinking, Elizabeth thought. The guy was obviously interested in Enid, and there was no reason to help him out in even the tiniest way. He was old enough to be their father!

Mel looked Enid up and down. "Well, Alex—"

"Sir," Elizabeth interrupted. "I can guarantee a hundred people."

"You can?" Enid and Mel said in unison.

Elizabeth felt a line of perspiration start to form at her forehead. Could she? What would happen if she said she'd have a hundred partyers and then only seventy showed? Mel would probably want even more money. But she couldn't back out now. She had to do this thing the right way—for Jessica.

"I can," Elizabeth said firmly. "Now let's talk money."

Winston stood between two tables at the Dairi Burger that night, gesturing grandly as he drew near the punch line of the funny story he was telling to a group of SVH students. "But Maria's father didn't know her little sister had been playing with his briefcase—"

"Winston!" Maria Santelli protested.

He held up a hand and continued. "Just a second, honey. I'm almost finished—"

"But—"

"And then Peter Santelli, the mayor of Sweet Valley, opens his briefcase in front of the entire city council," Winston explained dramatically, "and instead of budget recommendations, the only thing inside is Mr. Ted, the ratty old terry cloth teddy bear that Maria sleeps with!"

"A teddy bear?" Jessica shrieked, obviously enjoying the joke at the expense of her fellow cheerleader.

Maria blushed bright pink, and Winston realized, with a sickening lurch of his stomach, that he'd committed a grave mistake.

34

"A teddy bear. How sweet," Lila said coolly, one eyebrow arched with amused derision. "I'm sure the two of you are very happy together, Maria."

Bruce hooted with laughter. "You sleep with a terry cloth teddy bear, Santelli? That is *so* elementary school!"

Maria Slater nudged the other Maria sympathetically. "Lila and Bruce sleep only with *mink* teddy bears," she explained, sparking a few chuckles. Another ally, Olivia Davidson, was casting Winston a dark glare while patting his girlfriend's arm from across the table in a show of solidarity.

Winston wondered just how much trouble he was in. The four girls' reactions were divided. But Ken and Aaron's faces were red with suppressed laughter. *At least all the guys are with me*, Winston thought. Well, except for Todd. For the last half hour Todd had been staring at a plate of onion rings as if they were a trigonometry problem. Winston doubted that he'd heard a word of the conversation.

Winston's girlfriend stood up, her dark hair swinging around her face, and grabbed his upper arm in a pinching hold. "Egbert, we need to talk."

"I was afraid of that," he squeaked, wondering how a girl as petite as Maria could have such strong fingers.

Bruce, Aaron, and Ken grinned knowingly as Maria pulled Winston away from the two tables in the front section of the Dairi Burger. She dragged him to the back of the room and practically threw him into a corner booth. Then she flounced into the seat across from Winston and glared at him over the table. A gulf of silence stretched between them.

"You're having an expression," he said weakly.

"And you're having a memory lapse!" she exploded. "I told you about Mr. Ted in strict confidence. You promised you'd never tell anybody! Did that promise just slip your mind?"

"I'm sorry, Maria. You know how I get when there's a funny story to tell. Everything else just sort of flies out of my brain, and I—"

"And you broadcast my intimate secrets to all our friends, in the middle of the Dairi Burger! Of all the insensitive, boneheaded stunts—"

"I'm sorry, Maria. I guess I wasn't thinking."

"Obviously not," she said. "Your mouth was moving. For you that seems to preclude any brain activity."

"I said I was sorry." He reached across the table to take her hand in his, but she slapped it away.

"You're sorry now," Maria repeated. "And that's

supposed to make it OK that you embarrassed me in front of everyone? Being sorry after the fact is pointless!"

"No, it's not. It's totally pointy."

"The only thing pointy around here is your head!" Maria griped.

Winston made another grab for her hand, and this time he grasped it in his before she could pull it away. "Guilty as charged," he said meekly.

"How can I trust you if you can't keep your big mouth shut? Do you have any idea how you've humiliated me? I have to go to school with these people every day!"

Winston shrugged. "Only for a few more weeks," he pointed out. "Over the summer I bet they'll forget all about Mr. Ted."

Maria glared. "Gee, I see Elizabeth and Enid coming in the door. Are you sure you don't want to run over and tell them about my teddy bear too? Or maybe you'd just like to call CNN?"

"OK, OK, so I was a jerk—"

"I won't argue with that," she said, looking away.

"I was a dweeb," he continued. "A mentally challenged space cadet. A nitwit to the nth degree."

"You forgot rude, crude, and socially un-acceptable," Maria added. Her mouth was still clenched, but its corners were pulling upward ever so slightly. Winston began to relax.

"Those are good adjectives," he told her. "Mr. Collins, English teacher to the world, would be proud of you."

"Here's a few more adjectives for you," Maria said. "How about obnoxious and reality impaired?"

"Absolutely. And a major brat too." He stroked his chin thoughtfully. "And cute?" he added, smiling the lopsided smile that always seemed to wear down her resistance. "Maybe just a little?"

"Not *that* cute," she said grumpily.

Winston took a deep breath. "What can I say? I failed Boyfriend 101, and I'm sorry. Now please, please, please, let me take the remedial class?"

Maria rolled her eyes and gave him a tight smile. "All right. I forgive you," she agreed, her voice calm but still chilly. "Just don't let it happen again."

Winston breathed a sigh of relief. He had a feeling the bullet he'd just dodged could have been fatal.

A Jamie Peters ballad was playing on the jukebox when Enid and Elizabeth walked into the Dairi Burger on Monday evening. Enid noticed Todd sitting at a table near the front with Aaron, Bruce, Jessica, and Lila. Elizabeth swept by him without turning her head to look at him. And Enid wasn't sure if Todd had seen them. His eyes never left his untouched plate of onion rings.

She wondered briefly why Todd was sitting there. He couldn't stand Jessica and Lila, and he was no good friend of Bruce's either. Most likely, she decided, he and Aaron had already claimed the table when the others joined them. At the adjacent table Maria Slater sat across from Olivia and Ken. Conversation and laughter seemed to be moving between the two tables, but Todd was in a world of his own. Enid steered Elizabeth quickly to a booth in the back of the room, next to one where Winston was having an intense discussion with Maria Santelli.

"You OK?" Enid asked Elizabeth.

Elizabeth's lips were set in a tight little line. She inhaled deeply, as if she'd been holding her breath since the moment she spotted Todd. "Yeah, I'm fine," she said in a resigned voice.

"Maybe you should try talking to him. Set things straight between you."

Elizabeth shook her head. "No, there's nothing to say. Todd will never forgive me after what I did to him. And the truth is, I'm not sure I want him to."

"You mean you wouldn't make up with him even if he wanted to?"

Elizabeth shrugged. "Maybe someday. I don't know. Todd was an important part of my life for a long time. Too long, maybe. Look at all the fights we've had in the past year."

"But you always got back together."

"Maybe we shouldn't have," Elizabeth said solemnly. "Maybe we need some time apart to think things through. We'll be seniors next year. Then college. It's a good time to reevaluate whether we really want to be together."

"I know," Enid said. "But not *dating* is one thing. Not *speaking* is something else. You'd both be happier if you could at least be friends."

"I'd like to, but Todd's not ready for that," Elizabeth replied sadly. "I have to give him time."

Enid nodded. She hadn't spoken with Todd lately. He was avoiding her as much as he was avoiding Elizabeth. But it was clear to anyone who knew him that he was listless and depressed. "What about Devon?"

"I'll never have another chance with Devon except as friends." She stopped long enough to give their soft drink order to the waitress. Then she took a deep breath. "But we're not here to discuss my lack of a love life."

"No, we're here to talk about the party of a hundred people!" Enid exclaimed gleefully.

Elizabeth groaned. "Do you really think we can swing that?"

Enid smiled at her best friend. She was feeling much more optimistic about the turnout for the twins' party now than she had earlier—for one big reason. "Whatever, Wakefield. You and Jess are, like, the two most popular people in our class. You'll get a hundred yeses, no problem."

"I hope so," Elizabeth said, perking up slightly. "I'll worry about the invite list later. What do you think we should do for music?"

Enid gestured across the room to leggy, blond Dana Larson, a striking junior who was the lead singer for a punk band. "I bet Dana would give you a discount since she's a friend."

"That would be awesome!" Elizabeth said. "Jessica loves their music."

"*Everyone* loves their music," Enid corrected. "Too bad old Mel wouldn't give you a better deal. I thought he would at least throw in a DJ."

Elizabeth rolled her eyes. "As if," she said. "I had no idea it would cost so much to rent the place for the evening." She laughed. "I bet we could have gotten a break if it had been *you* renting it instead of me!"

"Ugh! Don't remind me. I'm surprised he didn't ask for my number!" Enid exclaimed.

"Maybe if I call him and tell him where you live, he'll come down on the price."

"Don't you dare!" Enid cried.

"If you were a real friend, you'd offer to go out with him for me," Elizabeth said, her blue-green eyes twinkling.

Enid crumpled a napkin and threw it at Elizabeth. "Don't hold your breath, girlfriend," she said. "And without throwing myself at old Mel, renting the place seemed pretty steep to me."

"I can handle it since I told Mel we'll be doing the food ourselves," Elizabeth assured her. "I have cash in my savings account, and my grandparents sent birthday money."

"Are you sure you want to max out your savings that way?" Enid asked. "I thought you were saving for the down payment on a new Jeep."

Elizabeth shrugged. "I was. But by the time I can afford to buy another Jeep, I'll be making the payments with my social security checks. Besides, Jessica's been through a rough year. I want to make this birthday special for her."

"You're a great sister," Enid said. "Jessica doesn't appreciate you nearly as much as she should."

"I think she does. She just doesn't always realize that she does!" Elizabeth replied, laughing.

"Let me take care of the party decorations, Liz. Consider it a birthday present to you both."

"Thanks," Elizabeth said with a warm smile. "That will be a major help."

Enid's mouth twisted in thought. "I hate to bring this up after you've written Mel a check for the deposit," she said. "But have you felt Jessica out on her plans? What if she's doing something with Lila and Amy on the thirteenth? Or worse, what if she's throwing a party for *you*? That would put a hole in your one hundred."

"I hinted around this morning, trying to get the scoop," Elizabeth said. "She didn't come right out and tell me one way or the other, but I'd be surprised if she were planning a party. You know Jessica. She's not exactly Ms. Strategic Planner."

"I guess you're right," Enid agreed. "If Jessica wanted a party, her style would be to suggest having one together and then let *you* do all the work!"

Chapter 4

Jessica crouched down in the front seat as Lila slipped her lime green convertible out of the school parking lot at noon on Tuesday. She didn't want to get caught sneaking off campus with her birthday coming up. Being grounded for her big day would really put a wrench in her plans.

"The coast is clear," Lila said as she pulled into traffic.

"Cool," Jessica said, popping back up.

"What does Principal Cooper call what we're doing?" Lila asked, rolled her eyes. "'Leaving the grounds during school hours without authorization'? How utterly lame."

"If Chrome Dome weren't lame, he'd have no personality at all," Jessica pointed out as Lila stopped at a red light. "I don't know when he expects us to have a life if we're trapped at school all day."

"Besides, all we're missing is lunch," Lila said. "Mystery meat and soggy vegetables."

"And if we happen to arrive back a little late for chemistry class, I think we'll find the courage to go on."

"Did you call the cellist this morning?" Lila asked.

"Yes, and I booked the quartet for the thirteenth!" Jessica exclaimed. "Oh, I almost forgot—I couldn't leave her my telephone number. I mean, what if she calls and Liz answers the phone?"

"That would be *so* not fixable," Lila remarked.

"So I gave her the number of your cell phone instead!" Jessica told her.

Lila sighed deeply. "I suppose it's all right."

"I knew you wouldn't mind," Jessica said cheerfully.

"Let me guess," Lila began. "You're planning to use my number on the party rentals too."

"That's what best friends are for!"

"I thought best friends were for driving you to Valley Caterers to rent a tent because your sister's stupid ex-boyfriend drove your Jeep off a cliff."

"That too," Jessica admitted. "Best friends are kind of multipurpose."

"Sounds like a laundry detergent," Lila said. "How flattering. I just hope one of my purposes isn't to lend you money for all this."

45

"Never fear, O Rich but Stingy One. It's all taken care of."

"I suppose we're going to stop at the Union Bank on the way there and rob it, aiming our blow-dryers like guns."

"In a white dress?" Jessica protested, gesturing down at her linen halter dress. "No way. I've heard that the dye stuff they hide in the money leaves horrible stains!"

"Another teenager deterred from a life of crime," Lila said. "So, if we're not becoming master thieves, how will you get the money? Planning to sell a kidney?"

Jessica whipped a plastic card out of her purse. "Mom's credit card!" she said.

Lila's tweezed eyebrows arched high. "I can't believe she's letting you borrow that. Liz, maybe. But *you*?"

"She's not exactly letting me," Jessica acknowledged. "But I called Steven at SVU last night, and he said he'd lend me some money. I just have to get it from him to pay Mom—before her credit card bill comes."

"I see, O Poor but Resourceful One," Lila said as she parked the car in front of the party rental store. "But I thought we were keeping the party a secret from your whole family."

"We are," Jessica said. "I told Steven I needed the money to buy something special for Liz for our birthday."

"Good cover," Lila said as Jessica hopped out of her seat. "Remind me never to trust you."

"Moi?" Jessica asked innocently as she held the door to the shop open for her friend.

"Toi," Lila confirmed. She walked over to the counter and snapped her fingers at the petite saleswoman. "Service, please," Lila said haughtily.

"This isn't a restaurant," Jessica reminded her. She flashed her brightest smile at the middle-aged woman. "We'd like to rent a tent for a party. How much will that be?" Jessica asked.

The woman smiled kindly. "Well, that depends on the size, dear. How many people are you expecting?"

Lila frowned at Jessica. "Oh, at least five hundred," Lila said.

"What?" Jessica exclaimed. "I didn't know I was inviting the whole school."

"You're right," Lila said with a small nod. "Maybe if the party was for me—"

"Or me," Jessica interjected.

"Or *you*," Lila amended. "But we can't expect that kind of turnout for Elizabeth, can we?"

"But don't forget, it is *my* birthday too," Jessica reminded her friend. "Tons of people will show up just because my name is on the invitation."

"Ladies?" the saleswoman said. "Do you want to come back after you've discussed this more?"

"No," Jessica said, making a snap decision. "I'd like a tent for one hundred people."

"Only one hundred?" Lila asked incredulously.

"Some poor souls will just have to be left out," Jessica said with a shrug. She told the woman where and when she wanted the tent delivered and handed her the credit card. Jessica signed her mother's name on the sales slip and slid it across the counter.

"Wait a minute," the saleswoman said, comparing the card with the receipt. "This isn't the same signature."

Jessica felt her knees weaken. No salesperson had ever challenged her before when she'd used her mom's card—which she'd done quite often.

"You aren't Alice Wakefield, are you?" the saleslady asked, a challenge in her eyes.

"Of course she is," Lila snapped. "Right, Al?"

"Of course I am," Jessica repeated.

"Then let's see some other form of ID," the woman countered, holding on to the credit card.

Jessica felt her face go beet red. "I . . . uh . . . I left my wallet at my . . . um—"

"You know, young lady, credit card fraud is a federal offense." The nice woman suddenly looked like a prison warden. Jessica swallowed, imagining herself in one of those icky orange prisoner jumpers. "But I—"

"Oh, give it up, Jess," Lila said finally. She popped open her purse and slapped a platinum credit card down on the counter. The saleslady looked at the little piece of plastic dubiously.

"I suppose you *are* Lila Fowler," she said.

"Please," Lila said, sounding totally offended. The woman still compared the signatures. When the transaction was finished, Jessica bolted from the store into the warm afternoon sunshine.

"I can't believe I froze," she wailed. "I *never* freeze!"

"You owe me big time, Wakefield," Lila said, following her out. "We'll discuss your interest rate later."

"I do not owe you interest," Jessica protested, climbing into the passenger seat.

"You *so* do," Lila said, fastening her seat belt. "At this point I've risked detention by skipping school, supplied the music, *and* paid for the tent. Pretty soon I'm going to tell Liz that *I* threw her birthday bash."

Jessica slumped down in her seat as Lila peeled out of the parking lot. Great. Now she was in debt to Lila Fowler, which—she knew from experience—was not a fun place to be.

I sure hope Liz appreciates all the trouble I'm going through for her, Jessica thought grumpily.

"I know it's going to be awesome," Ken said that afternoon as he followed Olivia into the garage of her family's home, which she'd converted into an art studio. He couldn't believe how excited he was about the unveiling of his portrait. His palms were actually sweating. "I can't wait to see this!"

"I really, really hope you like it," Olivia said, her pretty hazel eyes eager but nervous.

Ken noticed that a smear of bright pink paint clung to the untamed brown curls above one ear. "I know I'm going to love it!" he assured her. "As much as I love you."

For a moment Ken thought of other girls he'd dated—girls like Jessica and Amy, girls who were part of the "jock" crowd he'd always hung out with at school. Girls who seemed, on the surface, to have a lot more in common with him than Olivia did. Girls who would die before they'd be seen spattered with paint. Olivia was different. She was creative and talented and brave enough to be herself, even when that meant defying convention and shaking people up. And she was constantly challenging Ken to explore his own untested creative impulses.

When they first met in an on-line chat room a few months earlier, Ken and Olivia had no idea of each other's identities, and Freeverse—Olivia's screen name—had captivated Ken with her honesty, sensitivity, and lyricism. After a whirlwind cybercourtship they'd met in person. And Ken had been dismayed to learn that the exotic free spirit he'd grown to love was Olivia Davidson, a girl he'd known since kindergarten without ever really noticing. She'd been just as upset to learn that Quarter—Ken's screen name, short for *quarterback*—was a football player, not a poet.

In the end they'd decided to give their virtual love a try in the real world. And Ken had never been sorry that he took the chance.

Olivia lifted a pile of coarse-textured paper from a metal folding chair that was splotched with green and yellow paint and left the paper in a stack in a corner of the cluttered room. She patted the back of the chair. "Sit down and close your eyes."

Ken grinned. "What'll you give me if I do?" He grabbed her around the waist and kissed her squarely on the lips. Olivia laughed at first but then settled into the rhythm of his long, slow kiss.

"That wasn't exactly what I meant when I told you to close your eyes," Olivia protested weakly after they'd both come up for air.

He wiggled his eyebrows comically. "You're the one who's been teaching me to be more impulsive." But he obeyed her orders and sat in the folding chair, eyes squeezed shut. "OK, I'm ready. Lay it on me!"

"Hold on a sec while I pull it out," Olivia said. He heard the sound of something bumping against her easel.

"Ready?" Ken asked.

"No! Don't you dare open your eyes yet! I have to put it in place on the easel so you get the best view."

"Come on, Livy. Patience is way overrated. I'm dying to see what I look like in oils."

"Acrylics, actually," she corrected him. "And I need just one more second . . . OK, you can look now. Ta-da!"

Ken opened his eyes and his stomach turned. He leaped from the chair, staring wildly at the canvas. "What the . . . what is *that*?"

"What do you mean?" Olivia was wide-eyed. "Isn't it obvious? It's a portrait of you."

"But—but I'm not wearing anything in it!"

"Of course not, silly. That's why they call it a nude." The canvas showed Ken, full-length, standing in a lush, junglelike setting, like Adam in the Garden of Eden.

"How the heck did you paint me in the nude? You've never seen me naked!" Ken's whole face was on fire.

Olivia shrugged. "I'm an artist. I used my imagination."

"But—"

"What's the big deal? It's not like I've never taken a life drawing class, with live models." Olivia had been granted special permission to take college-level classes at a local art school, where she'd already won several awards.

"But everybody's going to think that I . . . that you . . . that we . . ." Ken trailed off, covering his eyes with his hand for a moment.

"I don't care what everybody thinks. We're the only ones whose opinions matter," Olivia said calmly.

Her total cool only fueled Ken's indignation. "My opinion is that you had no right!" Ken shouted, furious. "You have to destroy that painting."

Olivia's face was turning as pink as the paint smear at her temple. "Destroy it? How can you even suggest such a thing? You know how hard I've been working on this!"

"It's an invasion of privacy!"

"It's an exploration of the beauty of the human body. Get over it, Ken. Artists have been painting nudes for hundreds of years."

Ken couldn't believe her condescension. "They haven't been painting *me!*"

"Why shouldn't someone paint you?" Olivia argued. "You're an athlete. You're in terrific shape. You have nothing to be ashamed of, Ken."

"You're right. I don't. Because nobody is ever

53

going to see that painting!" he shouted.

Olivia folded her arms across her chest, her expression defensive. "If you get down to the nitty-gritty, the rights to this painting belong to me, the artist. Legally you have no say in what I do with it or who I show it to."

Ken shook his head in disbelief. "Legally? Tell me this is all a joke," he pleaded. "You had no right to paint that! And you absolutely can't show it to anyone!"

"It's no joke! And you have no right to tell me what I can and cannot paint or who I can show my work to!" Olivia yelled.

"Are you telling me you would go ahead and let people see this *thing*—even after I asked you not to?"

"I don't hear you *asking* me anything," Olivia retorted. "What I hear is you ordering me around! You may call the plays on the football field, Mr. Hotshot Quarterback. But nobody tries to censor my art and gets away with it. Nobody!"

"I wonder how it's going with Olivia and Ken," Elizabeth remarked to Enid and Maria Slater as they walked down Main Street in downtown Sweet Valley on Tuesday afternoon on their way to the post office.

"How *what's* going with Olivia and Ken?" Enid asked, swinging the tote bag that held the one-hundred–plus party invitations she and Elizabeth had addressed. "Do they have a hot date today?"

"Olivia finished Ken's portrait," Maria told her. She glanced at her watch. "Right about now he should be at her house for the grand unveiling."

"I can't wait to see it," Elizabeth said, searching her purse for money for stamps. "Olivia is terrific with portraits. She always manages to capture the things about a person that you don't normally see."

"She's great with colors too," Enid said. "I'm going to ask her for some advice on decorating the Beach Disco for the birthday bash."

"Well, I'm leaving the decorations completely in your capable hands," Elizabeth told her. "Go wild, girl."

Maria pulled out an invitation and began studying it. Elizabeth looked at her, concerned.

"What is it, Maria?" she asked, stopping in the middle of the sidewalk. "Don't tell me there's something wrong with the invitations we printed from my computer."

Maria smiled. "I'm sure they're fine. I just thought I'd give them one last go-over before we mail them off. . . . Wait a minute—"

"What did we do?" Enid asked. "Did we misspell *Wakefield*? I knew something would get screwed up, with the twins' birthday falling on Friday the thirteenth."

"Chill out, girlfriends. It's OK," Maria assured them. "I just stressed for a minute when I saw the phone number. It's not Liz's, and I was afraid it was a typo—until I realized it's Enid's number."

Elizabeth sighed. "Is that all?" she asked with a giggle. "You nearly gave us both heart attacks! I was really hoping to live until my seventeenth birthday, you know."

"We used my number because we didn't want people RSVPing to the Wakefield house," Enid explained. "Our cover is totally blown if Jessica picks up the telephone—"

"And if there's a phone ringing anywhere within earshot, just try keeping Jessica away from it," Maria added. "I get your point."

A few minutes later the girls emerged from the post office after mailing the invitations.

"Keep your fingers crossed," Elizabeth said, stopping in front of the building to shove a huge roll of postage stamps into her purse. "Enid had better start getting *a lot* of phone calls, or I'm going to end up washing dishes for Mel to pay off my debt."

"My ear is ready and waiting," Enid joked.

"What are all those stamps for, Liz?" Maria asked. "I didn't know they came in rolls that big!"

Elizabeth shrugged. "I always have to buy them

in bulk to compensate for the ones Jessica swipes from my desk. I swear, that girl never plans ahead—"

Enid nudged her into silence. "Ex-boyfriend alert!" she hissed.

Elizabeth froze. Devon Whitelaw was crossing the street toward them. As he reached the curb he looked up and stopped short.

"Uh, hi, Devon," Elizabeth said, wondering if her face was turning pink. She gazed at her former boyfriend, who stared at her intently, running a hand through his thick, dark brown hair as if he wasn't sure what else to do with his fingers.

"Hey, Devon!" Maria cried out in a breezy voice. "So, you have feet after all. Not just wheels. Where's that Harley-Davidson you're usually physically attached to?"

"I, um, parked it across the street," he said, but his slate blue eyes were still on Elizabeth. *He's still mad at me,* she realized with a sinking heart. *He'll never forgive me for deceiving him at the prom by dumping him on my sister while I danced with Todd.*

They were only supposed to be friends now, but Elizabeth's heart was racing at the sight of his rugged, angular features and his lean, muscular frame. "I haven't seen you around much lately," she said. "Busy studying for finals?"

Devon shrugged. "Yeah. Studying. Mr. Collins is socking us with Joyce, Hamlet, *and* Hemingway on the exam. You know."

"So, what brings you to this part of town?" Enid asked him.

"Just gettin' some stuff done. You?"

"I'm, um, planning a party for Friday the thirteenth," Elizabeth told him. Her heart was pounding loudly in her ears. *Just invite him,* her mind shouted. "It's a surprise birthday party for Jessica. We just put the invitations in the mail."

"Oh, yeah?" he asked, staring at her speculatively, his forehead wrinkled.

"You're invited," Elizabeth blurted, sounding moronic even to her own ears. "I mean, all our friends are. I hope you'll come. It's going to be a lot of fun."

Devon nodded tersely. "I'll check my calendar."

Elizabeth felt like kicking herself. Could that invitation have been more impersonal? And could his answer have been more cold?

Fifteen minutes later Devon roared through town on his motorcycle. "All her friends are invited," he muttered aloud into the wind. For a moment back there he'd thought she was going to invite him to her party as her date—not as just another friend. "Friends. Is that what we are now?"

In his head Devon knew it was true, but he sure wished someone would explain it to his heart. Every time Devon saw Elizabeth's gold blond hair and perfect figure, he wanted to grab her in his arms and kiss her. Even if they were in public. Even if they were chatting with her friends on the sidewalk in front of the post office. She was so smart and understanding and totally amazing, the only girl in town who had been interested in him for who he was rather than what he looked like or how much money he'd inherited when his parents died.

When his feelings for Elizabeth threatened to overwhelm him, Devon choked them back. He forced himself to remember every detail of that ghastly prom night, of Elizabeth showing up with Wilkins when she was supposed to be Devon's date. Of Elizabeth gazing into Wilkins's eyes.

Devon gunned the motor, feeling a cold, dull anger well inside him. "If Liz wants to be 'just friends,' then that's exactly what we'll be to each other," he resolved aloud. "She'll never see another shred of emotion out of me."

Chapter 5

Tuesday evening Jessica and Lila sat cross-legged in Jessica's cluttered bedroom, addressing envelopes. They had cleared a place to work by pushing aside part of the jumble of belts, scarves, and textbooks that always covered the floor. And Jessica had given in to Lila's fear of getting dog hair on her outfit and had banished the Wakefield's dog, Prince Albert, to the kitchen.

"You forgot to buy stamps," Lila told her.

Jessica jumped to her feet. "No biggie. Elizabeth always keeps a stash in her room."

"Convenient," Lila remarked behind her as Jessica negotiated the piles of clothes on the floor and then skipped through the twins' bathroom and into Elizabeth's room. Following her,

Lila stopped just inside the door, shaking her head. "Looking at the difference in your rooms, I can hardly believe you're even related, let alone identical twins."

"I know," Jessica agreed, rolling her eyes at Elizabeth's off-white walls, neatly made bed, cream-colored carpeting, and orderly desk. "I don't know how Elizabeth can stand to live in this place. It looks like a hospital ward."

"And yours looks like a psycho ward," Lila said, strolling to the center of the carpet as if she owned the room. "You've got to admit, your purple walls were an . . . *aggressive* choice."

"I like purple! Do you have a problem with that?" Jessica demanded, shuffling through the contents of her sister's desk. "And I love my room! I don't know how Elizabeth ever finds anything, the way she hides it away in drawers and things. It makes more sense to leave things out in plain sight, like I do, so you can see where they are."

"It makes even more sense to let the servants straighten up," Lila said. She picked up a nail file from Elizabeth's bedside table and began working on her manicure. "It makes them feel useful."

"You're a real humanitarian, Lila."

"Don't ever say that!" Lila ordered. "Not even in jest."

"Sorry, wouldn't want to wreck your hard-won reputation," Jessica said, reaching behind a perfectly aligned stack of notebooks. "Voilà! I've hit pay dirt." She held up a roll of stamps. "We are now in the mailing business."

"You're getting off pretty easy for this party," Lila began as they headed back through the bathroom to Jessica's room. "You got stamps from Elizabeth, a jazz quartet from Fowler Enterprises, money from me—"

"Money from *Steven*," Jessica corrected. "I'm paying you back as soon as he gets here and—"

"Even the original idea for the party came from me!" Lila concluded, talking over Jessica.

Jessica folded her arms across her chest. "In your dreams!"

Lila looked smug. "Don't deny it. You and Amy were talking about hamburgers or bowling or something. I was the one who came up with the idea of having an elegant jazz party on the beach."

"No way! You wanted to auction off men. I dreamed up this party all by myself!" Jessica couldn't remember the exact details of the conversation, but an idea so brilliant couldn't have come from any mind but her own.

"Don't you remember? I said it should be elegant instead of dull, and then I had my flash of inspiration."

"That flash was when your brain shorted out," Jessica said. "You may have used the word *elegant* first, but I was the one who turned a simple little adjective into an earth-shattering entertainment concept."

"You're delusional, Wakefield."

"*You* are the expert on delusions," Jessica said. She sat in the cleared space on the floor and pulled over a box of envelopes and a stack of invitations. "By the way, did I tell you I put your cell phone number on these invitations for RSVPs?"

"Thanks for asking me first," Lila huffed.

"Well, I couldn't exactly use my own phone number!" Jessica pointed out. "Not with Elizabeth on the same line."

"You and Liz are going to owe me big time. I loathe playing secretary."

Jessica shrugged. "So get the maid to take the calls. Besides, it's not like playing secretary. It's more like playing social director."

"Much better," Lila said sarcastically.

Jessica laughed. "Come on, slave. Let's get this over with before Liz takes her daily inventory and realizes her stamps are missing."

"This is a total nightmare." Lila stood in front of her locker at school before homeroom on Friday, holding an invitation in each hand. "Amy!" she screeched, catching a glimpse of her friend's long blond hair amid the crowded hallway. "What are we going to do about this?"

"Gee, Lila, I don't know," Amy replied. "Can you be a little more specific?"

"Didn't you get the invitations?" Lila asked. "Jessica's throwing Liz a surprise birthday party at one end of the beach, and Elizabeth is throwing Jess a surprise birthday party at the Beach Disco, on the other end of the beach. And they're both at eight o'clock, a week from tonight!"

"Jessica is our friend, not Liz," Amy pointed out. "We helped her plan the jazz party. I say we go to that one."

"But that party's for Liz! The other one is in Jessica's honor!"

"You're right. I hadn't thought about it that way. And I bet practically everyone we know got invited to both."

"Friday the thirteenth could be a major disaster," Lila said. "We have to find a way to fix this."

"Maybe we can get one of the twins to reschedule," Amy suggested.

"I don't see how without blowing the surprise." Lila slumped back against her locker.

"Well, what do *you* think we should do?" Amy asked.

"I don't have a clue," Lila admitted. She thought for a moment. "If my father faced this kind of conflict at work, the first step he'd take is to call together some of his best people for a brainstorming session."

"High noon in the cafeteria?"

Lila nodded. "A boardroom would be better, but the lunchroom will have to do."

"I guess we should just round up the usual suspects," Amy remarked.

"In particular I want Maria Santelli there," Lila said. "She likes both twins. Besides, she's a student council officer and her father's mayor, so she knows how to organize things. She'll be good for logistical details."

Amy nodded. "Yeah, the boring stuff. She's great at keeping track of our cheerleading schedules."

"Maria's in my homeroom, so I'll make sure she's with us. You talk to whichever cheerleaders you think we should include and anyone else who seems like a good bet."

"What about Liz's geeky friends?" Amy asked.

"Until we decide what to do, it's safer to leave them out of this. We have to be sure Jessica's interests are represented!"

"She had better appreciate all the trouble we're going through," Amy said.

"Especially a few months from now," Lila added, "when it's time for her to plan a surprise party for *my* seventeenth birthday!"

Bruce walked into the cafeteria and collided with Penny Ayala. Before he could even shout, his backside hit the hard linoleum floor, sending a sharp pain down his side.

"I'm so sorry!" Penny dropped to the ground and started picking up Bruce's books, his comb, his cell phone.

"Why don't you watch where you're going?" Bruce demanded, grabbing his stuff from her hands. It wasn't until that moment that he realized Penny was crying—hard.

"Penny, what's wrong?" Bruce asked, holding her elbow and helping her stand up. She pulled a tissue out of her crocheted bag and held it to her face.

"Like you care," Penny said through her tears. Bruce winced. He deserved that. In all the years he'd been in the same classes with Penny, he'd barely even looked at her, let alone spoken to her. But she was a nice girl, and he wasn't about to leave her blubbering at the cafeteria entrance.

"Well, if there's anything I can do . . . ," he said.

"There's nothing anyone can do. Harvard rejected

me!" Penny blurted. Bruce froze. He hadn't just heard that. Penny sniffled loudly, crumpling and re-crumpling the tissue in her hand.

"Harvard rejected *you?*" Bruce asked. His heart was pounding.

"Thanks for sounding so shocked," Penny said, leaning against the wall. "That was the only school I wanted to go to. I've dreamed about it my whole life."

Penny Ayala rejected from the school Bruce wanted . . . no . . . *needed* to get into? Straight-A, editor-of-the-school-paper, never-been-to-detention-in-her-life Penny? He must have heard wrong.

"Penny, are you sure?" Bruce asked, trying to control his ragged breathing. Images of four years of his own mediocre report cards flashed through his mind.

"Am I sure?" Penny let out a slight laugh. "My mom just read me the letter." She gestured limply at the pay phone. "If she was kidding, that's one cruel joke to play on your daughter."

"I think I'm gonna be sick," Bruce said. His stomach was churning, and sweat formed on his palms and along his hairline.

"Join the club," Penny said. She wiped under her eyes with the back of her hand. "Thanks for stopping, Bruce. I think I'm gonna head for the bathroom and clean myself up."

"OK," Bruce muttered. Penny brushed past him, and Bruce braced a hand against the wall for support. He took a deep breath and let it out slowly.

"If Penny didn't get in, I don't have a snowball's chance in hell," he said to himself. "This is all bad."

"OK, this is all sounding pretty good," Maria Santelli announced in the cafeteria at lunchtime after a half hour of brainstorming about the double-party dilemma. She ripped off a piece of her brownie and popped it in her mouth. "If we can pull this off, I think we really will save the twins' birthday."

Along with Maria, Lila, and Amy the group included cheerleaders Annie Whitman, Sara Eastbourne, and Jade Wu as well as Aaron Dallas and Barry Rork. Luckily Elizabeth was eating outside in the courtyard with Maria Slater and Enid, while Jessica had been called to Ms. Dalton's room to discuss her study strategy for the upcoming French final—a meeting Ms. Dalton had insisted on. Maria had been relieved to see there'd be no chance of the twins' over-hearing their conversation.

"Secrecy is totally necessary," Lila said. Maria noticed her throwing a pointed glance at Amy, who was one of the biggest gossips in school. "We can't tell anybody what we're planning—"

"Except for the people we already discussed," Maria concluded.

"Right," Lila said. "But nobody else. The sabotage parts won't work unless The Plan is a complete secret."

"The Plan?" Barry asked.

Jade shrugged. "Why not?" said the petite Asian American girl with a toss of her long black hair. "We have to call it something without giving away what we're talking about."

"Who's going to deal with the music part?" asked Sara, a smart, popular junior who—along with Jade—was one of the best dancers in the school.

"I will," Lila said. "Along with you-know-who."

"I still don't see how we'll get Jessica to—," Aaron began.

"That's the part I'm looking forward to most!" Amy replied. "It'll be awesome watching her squirm!"

"You'll take care of the site coordination?" Maria asked Amy.

Amy saluted. "You can count on me, Lieutenant."

"What about Mr. and Mrs. Wakefield?" Annie asked, her green eyes wide with excitement. She was a small, dark-haired sophomore whose family had moved in next door to the Wakefields earlier that year. "Will we need their help for any of this? If you need me to, I can—"

"Leave the parental issues to me," Lila interrupted. "I can handle old Ned and Alice."

Jade shook her head. "But won't Elizabeth think—"

"Probably," Maria said with a shrug. "But there's nothing we can do. She'll get over it when she sees the results."

"How are we going to spread the word without letting the wrong people know?" Barry asked.

Lila started to answer but caught sight of something over Maria's shoulder, and her voice trailed off. Instead she leaned close to Barry and whispered something in his ear.

"Winston!" Maria exclaimed loudly, turning to see what had made Lila clam up. Before her approaching boyfriend could see it, she shoved her lunch tray over the clipboard she'd been using for taking notes.

"What's up?" Winston asked. "Planning a revolution?"

Lila threw Maria a questioning glance, and Maria shook her head ever so slightly. Normally she'd welcome Winston's input, but with his recent track record for keeping secrets, she didn't want him anywhere near The Plan.

"Close," Lila replied. "It's a corporate over-throw."

"Ah, somebody's finally staging a coup against Chrome Dome Cooper, our alleged principal," Winston said with a knowing nod. He pulled out an empty chair, spun it around, and straddled it. "I'm your man for espionage work." He faked a British accent. "Egbert. Winston Egbert."

"Sorry, Win," Maria said as nonchalantly as she could. "The job's already filled."

"But not by someone with my qualifications," Winston protested. "I've seen every rerun of *Get Smart* at least six times. I can recite whole scenes of *The Man from U.N.C.L.E.*!"

"The man from where?" Annie asked.

Winston snorted. "I can see that someone was raised in a culture-free environment."

"That's culture?" asked Jade, whose tastes ran more to classical ballet.

"Winston knows every useless bit of trivia from television shows nobody else under thirty has ever heard of," Amy told her.

"And his mother is so proud," Lila said.

"The truth is, we're a little busy, Winston," Maria told him.

He held up his hands. "Say no more. I under-stand. I'll just sit here and swipe leftovers from everyone's lunches, and I swear I will not say a word."

"Egbert, we need some privacy," Barry told him.

"We're working on, um, a class project!" Annie chimed in.

"But you're all in different classes," Winston reminded them. "Annie and Jade are sophomores, Barry's a senior, and the rest of you are juniors. There isn't a single course that you're all taking together."

Maria sighed in frustration. "Winston, can we talk about this later?" she asked. "Lunch is almost over, and we're not finished with our discussion yet."

"So talk among yourselves! I'm not stopping you."

"Yes, Egbert, you are!" Amy said. "Would you please go crawl back into whatever hole you came out of so that we can finish firming up our plans for The Plan?"

"Amy!" Lila cried.

"Don't wig out on me!" Amy said. "We agreed to call it The Plan so nobody would know what we were talking about it if they heard us mention it! He doesn't know anything!"

"That's an understatement," Lila replied.

Winston's eyebrows shot up to his forehead.

"The Plan?" he asked, rubbing his hands together in anticipation.

"Winston, will you please just leave us alone?" Maria cried, louder than she'd meant to. Heads turned at neighboring tables.

Winston dropped his class clown facade, and his expression was troubled. "Maria, are we having issues I don't know about?"

"You know exactly what issue this is about," she insisted.

"Oh, I get it." Winston looked hurt. "This is about that teddy bear thing. You don't trust me!"

"Teddy bear?" Barry asked.

Maria felt a twinge of guilt at Winston's betrayed expression but reminded herself that it was his own fault. "You haven't given me much reason to trust you lately."

She noticed that Amy, Lila, and Barry were watching the exchange as if it were a boxing match. Annie, Jade, Sara, and Aaron were staring at the table. Winston noticed too. He rose to his feet, grabbed Maria's arm, and pulled her out of the cafeteria.

Winston blinked at the bright sunlight in the courtyard outside the cafeteria doors. As soon as his vision cleared he gazed helplessly into Maria's

73

beautiful, angry face. "I thought you loved me!"

"I do love you, Winston! But what do you expect after you've spilled the beans so many times?"

"If this is about that stupid teddy bear you're sleeping with—"

"Mr. Ted is not stupid!" Maria cried, her small hands balling into fists at her sides. "And it's not just about him. You told my sister I got a C on my English paper last week, and she told my folks. You told Randy Mason what I said in private about Penny Ayala having a crush on him. You told—"

"Those were all accidents," Winston protested. "I'd never tell anyone a secret that really counted!"

"How am I supposed to know that anymore?" Maria wailed.

"You're supposed to trust me! I can't believe you'd sit there in the middle of the cafeteria and broadcast to everyone—to my friends—that you don't trust your own boyfriend enough to tell me about this top secret plan of yours."

Maria shook her head. "I can't tell you about that!"

"Because you don't trust me."

"Of course I trust you," Maria insisted. She stopped. "Well, with some things."

"We're supposed to be a couple!" Winston said, clenching his jaw. "We're supposed to be able to tell each other anything!"

"I wish I could tell you. It's not my fault you've got a mouth the size of the Pacific Ocean!"

"Fault?" Winston asked. "Are you saying this argument is all *my* fault?"

"I'm saying you need to work on keeping your mouth shut if you want people to trust you with their secrets."

"So I was right. You don't trust me! Am I supposed to pretend everything is peachy between us when I know you don't trust me anymore? How can we go on seeing each other like there's no change in our relationship?" He stopped, realizing what he'd said. *How can we go on seeing each other?*

Maria's eyes were filled with tears. "Maybe we can't," she said softly. She wiped her eyes with her sleeve, spun on her heel, and ran back into the cafeteria—leaving Winston standing alone, blinking in the white sunlight.

Chapter 6

After dinner that night Jessica stood in the Wakefields' cheerful, Spanish-tiled kitchen, petting the dog and watching Elizabeth rinse the pasta bowls in the sink. She eyed her sister speculatively. Everything was going exactly as she'd hoped. As far as she could tell, Elizabeth didn't have an inkling about the jazz party on the beach.

"Excuse me!" Elizabeth said. "I wouldn't want to interrupt your deep thinking, but we're supposed to be cleaning up the kitchen *together*. As in, *both* of us doing the work."

Jessica shrugged. "We are," she said. "I'm supervising. Mom and Dad always said we should aspire to leadership positions."

"I see. How about leading the glassware into the dishwasher?"

"You know, Liz, I prefer a more modern style of leadership," Jessica said with a smile. "Instead of forcing the glasses to blindly follow orders, I'm motivating them to really *want* to get clean."

Elizabeth nodded. "And when they want it badly enough, I suppose they'll jump into the dishwasher on their own?"

"It will be a testament to my excellent leadership skills."

"How progressive of you," Elizabeth remarked. "It's unfortunate that leading by consensus takes so long. By the time the glasses have made up their minds to feel motivated enough, you'll be late for your date with Danny Porter tonight."

Jessica whipped out the top rack of the dishwasher and shoved the nearest glass into it. "You know, there's something to be said for good old-fashioned discipline too." Prince Albert looked up with what Jessica thought was a bored expression and slowly padded over to his doggie bed in the corner, where he turned himself around three times before settling down.

Elizabeth grunted and began wiping the tile counter. "Especially when it's Friday night and you have a date."

"Friday?" Jessica asked. "Is it Friday already? That means our birthday is only one week away. Hard to believe it's coming so quickly. But you're so good at thinking ahead. I bet you've been planning for it for ages."

Elizabeth gave her a long, appraising stare. "What kind of planning?"

"Oh, you know. Birthday things. Like, oh, presents and parties and stuff. Whatever," Jessica answered nonchalantly.

"No, Jessica," Elizabeth said. "I'm not going to tell you what I'm getting you for our birthday."

"If you tell me what it is, I'll finish cleaning the kitchen all by myself!" Jessica wheedled.

"That's a tempting offer, seeing as how I've already done almost all the work."

"I'm curious, not stupid!"

Elizabeth laughed. "Patience never was your strong point."

"Come on, Liz!" Jessica hoisted herself up to sit on the counter. "I'll know in a week anyhow. What difference does it make if you give me a teeny little hint?"

Elizabeth just smiled placidly and poured dishwasher detergent into the compartment inside the door of the machine.

"You're such a brat," Jessica complained.

"We'll actually be high-school seniors soon," Elizabeth said a minute later, staring around the kitchen with a wistful expression on her face. "And then we'll be leaving here to go to college."

"I can't wait!" Jessica cried. "But you don't look very happy about it."

"Oh, I'm looking forward to going to college," Elizabeth said, a faraway expression in her eyes. "So many new things to learn about . . ."

"Like fraternity parties, freedom from curfews, and having my own credit card!" Jessica swung her legs happily.

Elizabeth gave her a little smile and shook her head. "You know that isn't what I meant."

"Whatever it is you mean, you sure look bummed out about it."

"I'm not!" Elizabeth said. "Well, only a little. Mostly I look forward to growing up and being more independent. But look around you, Jessica. This has been our home for as long as we can remember. Aren't you going to miss it? And Mom and Dad?"

Jessica shrugged. "It'll still be our home even if we're away at school somewhere. And Mom and Dad will still be here for us."

"I know, but it won't be the same. I've always loved this house."

"What's the big deal? It's not like it's Fowler Crest or something."

"I know you don't mean that," Elizabeth said. She

gestured around the bright, spacious kitchen. "Think about all the good times we've had in this house: hosting parties out by the pool, gabbing on the phone with friends, standing here in the kitchen while you palm your chores off on me. . . ."

Jessica caught site of the golden retriever sleeping in the corner and chuckled at a sudden memory. "Hiding Prince Albert in the basement for a week because we were afraid to tell Mom and Dad we adopted a puppy!"

"What about school dances? Sometimes I think we have the most fun here at home before the guys even show up," Elizabeth said slowly, her eyes shining. "Racing around our bedrooms together, borrowing things from each other's closets, and zipping up each other's gowns . . ."

Jessica sighed. Elizabeth was talking way sappy, but she was right. The house was full of memories, and most of them were funny or exciting or at least pleasantly familiar ones. "OK, so we'll miss the house when we go off to college, but isn't it a little early for major nostalgia jags? We have a whole twelve months before high-school graduation."

"I know it's premature," Elizabeth said with a laugh. "I don't know why I'm getting so gushy about leaving home. I guess having our birthday next week is making me think about growing up."

"Speaking of our birthday," Jessica began, hoping Elizabeth's guard was down, "I don't suppose this sisterly bonding has made you more likely to give me a teensy little hint about my present?"

"Why? It's not like *you've* told me what *my* present is!" Elizabeth pointed out. "Or that you're planning anything special for the evening."

"Why should I tell you when you're too mean to tell me?"

Elizabeth scrubbed at the spaghetti pot in an apparent show of nonchalance, but Jessica saw a gratifying glimmer of curiosity in her eyes. "You've never been able to keep a secret in your life!" Elizabeth reminded her. "Why start now?"

If she couldn't get any information out of her sister, Jessica decided she could at least give her a dose of her own medicine. "You'd be surprised at how well I can keep a secret when I feel like it," Jessica said cryptically.

Elizabeth dropped the show of indifference. "What secret?"

"OK, I'll tell you," Jessica said, watching Elizabeth's eyes light up. She took the clean spaghetti pot from Elizabeth and focused for a moment on wiping it with a dish towel. She grinned. "I'll tell you—*a week from tonight!*"

"Jessica!" Elizabeth protested.

Jessica bent down to place the spaghetti pot in a cupboard. Then she rose to her feet, giving her sister what she hoped was an irritatingly sweet smile. She sauntered toward the doorway, then turned and tossed the dishcloth at Elizabeth. "Patience," Jessica remarked, "never was your strong point."

"You should have heard Jessica after dinner last night," Elizabeth said to Olivia and Maria Slater on Saturday afternoon as they shopped for party supplies at the bulk grocery store on Route 1, just outside of town. "She's rabid to know what I'm planning for our birthday!"

Maria glanced up from a display of potato chips. "What about our birthday extravaganza? Do you think little sister has a clue about it?"

"I'm sure she doesn't," Elizabeth said. "She was giving me the third degree about what kind of present I'm buying her."

"Maybe you should skip a present altogether," Olivia said bitterly. "She probably wouldn't be grateful no matter how much time and effort you put into it."

Elizabeth stared at her. "That's harsh! Is something wrong, Olivia?"

"No, everything's fine," Olivia insisted, but her eyes had a faraway look. She picked up a bag of chips and studied the label.

Elizabeth glanced at Maria to see if she might know what was bothering Olivia. But Maria didn't appear to have noticed their friend's tone. She was staring at the shopping list as if it were written in Portuguese. Elizabeth decided Olivia would talk when she was ready. For now they had shopping to do. "Maria, do you think we should go for potato chips and onion dip or tortilla chips and salsa? We did invite a ton of people. Maybe I should get both?"

Maria glanced up quickly, as if startled. "Definitely not both. I don't know. You probably shouldn't buy either one for now."

"The party's less than a week away!" Elizabeth reminded her. "Why wait?"

"Uh . . . to give us more time to decide whether we want potato chips or tortilla chips," Maria said. "Right, Olivia?"

Olivia looked up quickly as if she'd been asleep and blinked twice at Maria. "Oh, right!"

"How much time do we need?" Elizabeth asked. "It's not exactly a life-or-death decision."

"Maybe you shouldn't serve food," Olivia suggested. "Everyone will be so busy dancing and listening to the band. Who has time to eat?"

"I'm with Olivia," Maria said quickly.

"Not serve food? We're not talking about a five-course gourmet meal! Just munchies. How can we have a party without munchies?"

Olivia shrugged. "It was just a thought."

"I think we should wait and buy the snacks closer to the end of the week," Maria said. "That way they won't have time to get grody before the party."

Elizabeth couldn't understand why her friends were acting so vague and unreasonable. "Hello! The party is six days away. Since when does a sealed bag of chips go stale in six days?"

Olivia and Maria stared at her blankly.

"What is it with you two?" Elizabeth demanded.

Maria shrugged. "Sorry I'm being indecisive. I'm just tired. I was up way too late last night, getting in some studying for the history final. It's hard concentrating on potato chips when you can barely keep your own eyes open."

"So we'll do chips later," Elizabeth decided, trying to hide her annoyance. "Who's up for a trip to the soft drinks aisle instead?"

"To tell you the truth . . . ," Olivia started, her voice trailing off.

"OK, I think I'm getting the picture," Elizabeth said after a moment. She reached into her purse and pulled out a folded slip of paper that Enid had given her a few days earlier. "Let's forget about food for now and talk about decorations."

"I thought Enid was the decorations czar," Maria said.

"She is, but since she couldn't come today, she gave me a list of what to buy. Olivia, she's counting on your artistic judgment to help us choose colors."

Olivia scowled. "Nobody else seems to trust my artistic judgment lately!"

Elizabeth put a hand on Olivia's shoulder and steered her to a quiet corner, and Maria followed along. "Olivia, what is it? And don't say you're studying too hard. Something's got you upset."

Olivia shook her head hopelessly. "Sorry. I know I've been showing some major attitude. My mood reeks, but I shouldn't take it out on you two."

"Just tell us what's wrong," Elizabeth urged.

"It's Ken. He hated the portrait."

"He hated it?" Maria asked, her eyes wide. "What's wrong with that boy? I've seen your work, girlfriend. You have some major talent."

"I was wondering why you'd been so quiet about what happened when he saw it on Tuesday," Elizabeth said.

Olivia's hands were clenched into fists. "I was too stunned to talk about it. I couldn't believe his reaction!"

"What's his problem?" Elizabeth asked. "Didn't he think it was a good likeness?"

Olivia gave a wry laugh. "More like *too* good. The thing is, I painted Ken as a nude. And he totally lost it."

"A nude portrait of Ken Matthews, Mr. Quarterback Bod?" Maria asked, a slow smile spreading across her face. "That I'd like to see!"

"Hey! Watch it! He's still my boyfriend," Olivia scolded. "I think."

Elizabeth felt her cheeks growing warm and wished she didn't blush so easily. "But Ken didn't pose for a nude portrait!" She gulped. "Did he?"

"Of course not," Olivia assured her. "I used my imagination."

"With a hunk like Ken for a boyfriend, I'd use my imagination too," Maria said with a laugh.

"Now he wants me to destroy the painting!" Olivia cried. "After all the hours I spent on it."

Maria patted her on the arm. "I can see why that would put your enjoyment on pause."

"But it's also understandable that he'd be upset," Elizabeth said, trying to be diplomatic. "I mean, if he thought that other people would see it."

"Are you saying you think I should destroy it too?" Olivia asked, her voice rising.

Elizabeth shook her head. "No, of course not. But if you're still planning to put it in the school art show, I can see why Ken is concerned—"

"I haven't even told him about the art show yet,"

Olivia admitted. "He was so freaked just seeing the portrait that I decided to let him chill out first."

"So has he chilled out?" Maria asked.

"No," Olivia replied. "He's just plain chilly. I tried to talk to him after school a few days ago, and I almost got frostbite."

Maria took a deep breath. "Don't take this wrong, Liv. But are you sure you want to press on with this art show thing? If it were me in Ken's place, I sure wouldn't want to be up there on the wall in all my altogether—if you know what I mean."

"Some of the finest masterpieces in the history of painting have been nudes!" Olivia argued vehemently. "Michelangelo, Manet, Gauguin . . . they all painted nudes!"

"What made you decide to paint Ken as a nude in the first place?" asked Elizabeth. "I thought you were doing a lot of abstract work lately."

Olivia thought for a moment. "It's hard to explain. I have been experimenting with abstract forms, but when I started thinking about painting Ken's portrait, that approach didn't feel right. I visualized the painting in a certain way, and that's how I painted it."

"And I guess you were happy with the way it came out?" Elizabeth asked.

Olivia nodded. "It's the best piece I've ever done."

"But Ken will feel dissed big time if you exhibit it," Maria said.

"He'll probably never speak to me again."

Elizabeth pursed her lips. "You have to decide if it's worth the trade-off. That's rough. Your chance to show your best work against Ken's fear of being embarrassed."

"It's more than a chance to show my work!" Olivia explained. "What's at stake is my integrity as an artist. I can't let anyone else's notions of propriety compromise my artistic vision!"

"But doesn't Ken have a right to privacy?" Maria asked.

Olivia pushed a tangle of brown curls off her forehead. "Of course he does," she replied slowly. "But Ken's right to privacy isn't being compromised. I'm not exposing him. I'm expressing my own, personal impression of him. It's not inflammatory or slanderous. I'm only trying to show the beauty of the human form."

"I guess Ken doesn't see it that way," Maria guessed.

"He doesn't have the right to tell me what to paint!" Olivia argued.

Elizabeth crossed her arms thoughtfully. "I think it's like when Principal Cooper tried to censor my newspaper article on sexual harassment in the schools."

"Exactly!" exclaimed Olivia, nodding gratefully. "When Mr. Cooper wouldn't let you print it in the *Oracle,* you didn't cave in and blindly obey him. You printed up your own newspaper!"

"There's one major difference," Maria pointed out.

"What's that?" Olivia asked.

"Chrome Dome wasn't Elizabeth's boyfriend."

Enid and Maria stared at each other over a plate of chocolate chip cookies at Enid's house. Invitations to both twins' parties also lay on the table between them.

"I managed to keep Liz from spending a fortune on party food yesterday," Maria said. "But she thinks I've completely lost it!"

Enid laughed. "She did mention something on the phone last night about you pulling a Hamlet over the life-or-death potato chips decision!"

"To dip or not to dip! That is the question," Maria intoned.

"So how did you keep her from buying all the food and stuff?"

"To be honest, Olivia deserves more of the credit than I do, even if it wasn't intentional.

She provided a distraction at exactly the right moment."

"What kind of distraction?" Enid asked.

"The double whammy—advice to the lovelorn, combined with a threat to freedom of expression."

"Ah, the Olivia-and-Ken saga."

"Seriously, I hate to see them on the skids. But that portrait they're fighting about sure helped sidetrack Liz from the party shopping!" Maria said, grabbing a cookie.

"That's our Liz. Hit her with a First Amendment issue or a friend in need, and everything else takes a backseat!" Enid laughed.

Maria nodded, chewing. "That's exactly what went down. But we can't sidetrack her forever, E. This party is only five days away! She's so organized, I'm surprised she didn't blow a fuse when she didn't get anything done today."

"I know. What we need is a plan. Any ideas?"

"Not a clue," Maria said with a sigh. "I just know that we can't let the twins go ahead with their parties for each other if they're each going to miss the one they're the guest of honor at!"

Enid raised one eyebrow. "There's something terribly ungrammatical about that sentence, but I won't even try to dissect it."

"The twins aren't the only problem," Maria began

a minute later. "Somehow all the guests would have to be at both parties at the same time too."

Enid propped her elbows on the counter and rested her chin in her hands. "Do you think we can perfect human cloning by Friday?"

"Don't even think about it!" Maria warned. "The only reason we're in this jam is because we've already got identical Wakefields."

"The rest of us could kind of go back and forth between the parties," Enid suggested. "A few minutes at the Beach Disco, a few minutes at the other end of the beach . . . But what do we do with Liz and Jess?"

"Do you think we can get one of them to cancel a party?" Maria asked.

Enid shook her head. "I don't see how. Not without spilling the lima beans." The phone rang and she rose to answer it, but her mother's voice called down from upstairs, saying she would pick it up.

"Too bad Olivia's so distracted about Ken right now," Maria said. "We could really use another creative mind."

"Enid!" called Ms. Rollins down the stairwell. "The phone's for you."

"Thanks, Mom!" Enid yelled back. "Who is it? Olivia?"

"It's Lila Fowler!"

Maria's eyes widened. "Since when are you and the Ice Princess chummy?"

Enid shook her head. "In all the years I've known Lila, I don't think she's ever called me," she said, reaching for the receiver. "Must be about the dueling parties."

"Hi, Lila," Enid said into the receiver. "Let me guess. You got the same two invitations everyone else got."

"Of course I did," Lila said, her voice sounding tinny through the phone line. "How could you let Elizabeth do this?"

"Do what? Plan a birthday party for her sister?" Enid asked, indignant. "I didn't know it was a felony. Besides, you let Jessica do the same!"

"That's different. Our party is going to be a classy affair."

"Get over it, Lila. You know Jessica would be totally psyched about the Beach Disco!"

"I suppose." Lila's weary sigh was audible through the phone. Enid imagined Lila pouting into her powder blue princess phone as she lounged on her satin-draped four-poster bed—probably manicuring her nails while she talked. She longed to share her speculation with Maria. Enid was far removed from Lila's inner circle of friends, but she'd seen the room a few times during parties at Fowler Crest.

"If you called just to complain about Elizabeth, I really have better things to do," Enid told her. "Like find a way to straighten out the twin parties and give them both a happy birthday."

"Luckily for you I've had some of my best people working on it," Lila said breezily. "And we have come up with . . . The Plan."

"Sounds ominous," Enid remarked. "The Plan for what?"

"The Plan for a successful birthday outcome, of course."

"You sound like you're planning a corporate merger," Enid joked.

"We are in a way. Life is three-fourths strategic planning, Enid," Lila answered dryly.

"And what's your strategic plan for handling a double-booked birthday?"

"It's a bit complicated," Lila began. "Though brilliant, if I do say so myself—"

"You *always* say so yourself."

"The fact is," Lila continued, raising her voice slightly, "we've found a way to be in two places at the same time."

Enid covered the receiver. "I spoke too soon," she told Maria. "Lila has figured out the secret of human cloning."

"Dr. Fowlerstein, I presume," Maria said in a

British accent. "Rats! There goes my shot at the Nobel Prize for party planning!"

"Enid, there's someone else there with you," Lila complained. "We need your help with The Plan, but it's on a strict need-to-know basis. Get rid of whoever's there."

Enid felt her face muscles clench. "Maria Slater is sitting here at my kitchen table, eating chocolate chip cookies. Wanna make something of it?"

"I suppose at Maria's height a few extra calories are easy to hide."

Enid stuck out her tongue at the telephone receiver, eyes crossed, and Maria laughed.

"So can I let Maria in on the deal?" Enid asked Lila dryly. "Or does telling her mean I'd have to kill her?"

"Yes, you can tell Maria," Lila allowed. "We need her help too. And a few other people."

"Help with what, already?" Enid asked, growing impatient.

"Help with The Plan, of course," Lila replied, in the tone of voice she might use to address a first grader. "Here's what we need you to do. . . ."

A few minutes later Enid hung up the phone and sank back into her chair, drained.

"You look like you could use one of these," Maria said, offering her a cookie.

"After a conversation with that snobby brat, I could use a dozen of them!"

"If that was about a way to save Friday the thirteenth, then you deserve at least that many," Maria told her. "But first give me details, girl. I need details. Did Lila Fowler and her lunatic friends come up with something workable? And what's our part in it?"

Enid nodded wearily and took a bite of cookie. "Yes, we do have a plan, and I think I just helped improve it some," she said. "I should be ecstatic. Our problems are solved. But what I feel is weird!"

"I bet you never envisioned yourself forming an alliance with the Fowl One!" Maria replied with a laugh.

"Never," Enid acknowledged. "It's like I've made a deal with the forces of darkness."

Chapter 7

Todd sat in his room Sunday evening, as perplexed as anyone by the invitations to two different, simultaneous parties for the Wakefield twins.

A month earlier the decision would have been hard enough: to support his girlfriend by going to the party she was hosting or to celebrate her birthday by going to the party Jessica was giving for her. Now that Elizabeth was no longer his girlfriend, the situation felt even stickier. As much as he hated to admit it, he still loved her. He'd always assumed he'd be there for her birthday. The thought of missing such an important day sent a fierce pain wrenching through his gut.

And now Enid was on the telephone describing some plan for allowing everyone to celebrate both twins' birthdays—a way for them all to be in two places at once.

"Enid, that's not even possible," Todd objected after she'd outlined The Plan. "It's not going to work."

"That's what I thought when Lila called to fill me in a half hour ago. But I've heard all the details, Todd, and I've thought it through. I think it'll be OK."

"*Lila* had something to do with this? No wonder it sounds so screwy."

"Give it a chance, Todd."

"The truth is, I'm not sure I want to go to either twin's party, let alone to both of them!" Todd said gruffly. "Not after the stuff Liz and Jess pulled on prom night. Dammit, Enid. You know what she did to me!"

Enid sighed. "Yes, I do. But that's history now. Elizabeth probably wouldn't want me to tell you this, but I know she wants to be friends with you. You're still important to her."

"She sure has a bonehead way of showing it," Todd mumbled. He sighed, sounding pathetic even to his own ears.

"It would mean a lot to her to have you at her birthday party, Todd. And I think it would mean a lot to you too."

"I don't know."

"Todd, she thinks you hate her," Enid said.

"Why shouldn't I hate her?" he replied, his voice rising an octave.

Enid was silent for a moment. "I don't know," she finally answered. "Maybe you should. But I know you, and I know Liz. And I have trouble believing that you *could* hate her, even after the way she treated you."

Todd took a deep breath. "You're right. I don't hate her. It's just too hard to see her right now."

"I understand how you feel," Enid said sadly. "Look, I won't expect your help with any of the planning. I don't know why Lila and her friends thought you'd be willing to help anyhow."

"Don't expect me, *period.*"

"As for coming that night," Enid continued as if Todd hadn't spoken, "I'm not taking no for an answer. Not yet."

"Enid—"

"Just think about it!" Enid insisted.

After he hung up, Todd sat silently, staring out his bedroom window at the growing darkness. Enid was right. On the one hand, he'd give anything to be with Elizabeth on her birthday. On the other hand, seeing her that night would just about kill him. One thing was for certain. Spending the whole summer trying to avoid Elizabeth in a town as small as Sweet Valley would turn him into a basket case before the start of his senior year.

"That's it!" he decided aloud. "It's time to come up with a plan of my own."

That evening Olivia was relieved when Ken's father opened the door of the Matthews house in response to her knock. *If it had been Ken there,* she thought as she followed Mr. Matthews inside, *he probably would have slammed the door in my face.*

After Ken's father retreated to the kitchen, Olivia trudged slowly up the stairs, biting her lip. She had no idea how this conversation was going to turn out, but it was bound to be unpleasant.

She stood outside the half open door of Ken's room, listening to the hum of his computer and the click of his fingers on the keys. She smiled, remembering that he'd been sitting right there at that keyboard when they first fell in love.

"Ken?" she asked in a soft voice, standing in the doorway. "Can I talk to you?"

Ken looked up from the screen, obviously startled.

She nodded toward the computer. "I hope you weren't in the market for another cybergirlfriend," she said with a wary laugh.

He returned her weak laughter. "I'm glad you came by," he said after an awkward silence.

Olivia felt her whole body relax. "Really?"

"Definitely," Ken said. He rose from his desk chair and leaned over to kiss her on the cheek. "I've been hoping you'd come to your senses and apologize."

"Apologize?" she asked, pulling away from his kiss. Suddenly she was tense again.

"Come on, Olivia. You're a reasonable person. You must understand why I'm upset about that portrait."

Olivia closed her eyes for a moment, taking a deep breath. The last thing she wanted to do was explode in anger and start the two of them yelling at each other again. "I am very sorry that you were disappointed by the portrait," she said carefully.

"And?" he prompted.

Olivia raised her upturned palms. "And I hope we can agree to disagree on this one." *That's good,* she thought. Even Elizabeth Wakefield, the most diplomatic person she knew, couldn't have phrased it better.

Ken smiled. "I assume that means you'll take a knife to that portrait and no hard feelings."

"A knife?"

"You know, cut it up before anybody sees it."

Olivia couldn't believe how easily he could toss off comments about destroying a piece of art she'd thrown her entire soul into. "No, that's not what I meant," she said through clenched teeth.

"Then let's compromise," Ken suggested. "You don't have to slice it to shreds. Just shove it in the back of a closet somewhere, and I'll trust you not to show anybody."

"I'll do no such thing!" Olivia cried, her voice rising despite her efforts to control it.

"Do you mean you still plan to let people see it?" Ken demanded.

Olivia struggled to keep her voice from quavering with anger. "Ken, before the painting was even finished, I'd already entered it in the art show at school."

Ken's eyes deepened to a dark, opaque shade of blue, and he grabbed the edge of the desk as if to steady himself. "Tell me you don't mean that!"

"It's not the kind of thing I'd make up for kicks," Olivia replied.

"Oh, that's just prime. All your college art student buddies will be ogling me—"

Olivia shook her head and took a deep breath. This was not going to go over well. "Not the college, Ken. That portrait will be on display in the spring art show at Sweet Valley High."

"*What?*" A sheen of sweat broke out on Ken's face, and he sat down quickly. "This isn't happening," he whispered. "You can't put that up where all our friends will see it!"

"Yes, actually, I can," she said, crossing her arms in front of her.

"Who the heck do you think you are?" he shouted. "Do you have any idea how people will react when they see a picture of me in the nude?"

"What are you so worried about? The portrait makes you look good!"

"That's not the point!"

"There's nothing on that painting that your friends don't already know you've got!" Olivia pointed out. "The entire football team and every guy in your gym class has seen you undress in the locker room!"

"This is different!"

"Why is it different?"

Olivia watched a nerve twitch in Ken's temple as he struggled to control his rage. After a moment he exhaled deeply and responded in a quieter voice. "Remember about a week ago at the Dairi Burger?"

"What does the Dairi Burger have to do with anything?" Olivia asked, plopping down on the edge of the bed. She suddenly felt exhausted.

"At the Dairi Burger—on Monday, I guess," Ken began, "Winston blabbed to a bunch of us about Maria Santelli sleeping with a teddy bear. Remember what a jerk Patman was about it?

Remember what a hard time Lila and Jessica gave her?"

Olivia shook her head, perplexed. "I don't understand what Maria's teddy bear has to do with my portrait of you!"

Ken sighed impatiently. "Imagine Bruce, Lila, and Jessica's reactions but about a million times worse. Then multiply it by the number of people at school who know me and will see or hear about that portrait if it's in the art show!"

"Ken, this is ridiculous," Olivia said. Nobody in her college-level classes had such hang-ups about depicting the human body. She had thought Ken was mature enough to understand. "Look, the only reaction to a painting that matters is a person's reaction to it as *art*. Who cares about the rantings of a few immature dweebs who have no life?"

"I have to go to school with those immature dweebs!" Ken shouted, standing up and glaring down at Olivia.

She stood to meet his gaze. "Yes, but you don't have to sink to their level."

"Olivia, the bottom line is that if you exhibit that portrait where people can see it, I'll never be able to show my face—or anything else—in Sweet Valley again!"

"You always say you're proud of me for sticking

up for my ideals," Olivia told him. "We're talking about my artistic integrity!"

"Is your artistic integrity more important than my reputation?"

"I don't believe in reputations! People who worry about their reputations are people who will compromise their principles because they're afraid to make waves!" Olivia cried. "I can't do that. I *won't* do it!"

"I thought you loved me!" Ken shouted.

Olivia opened her mouth to retort but stopped. Ken's eyes looked so desperate. She took a deep breath and continued in a quieter tone.

"I do love you, Ken, but that doesn't give you the right to censor my art. If *you* really loved *me*, you wouldn't want me to abandon my ideals."

"I just want you to abandon that god-awful painting!" Ken countered. "If you really loved me, you wouldn't put me through this!"

Olivia's blood boiled all over again. "Is that a threat?"

"No," Ken replied. They both turned at the sound of a footstep on the stairs. Their argument was attracting his father's attention. Ken's voice lowered to a cold, steely pitch. "It's not a threat. It's an ultimatum. If you want to see me again, you'll pull the nude portrait from the art show!"

Olivia gasped, stunned that the guy she loved would insist on such a sacrifice from her—and, even worse, act as if it was no sacrifice at all. "You don't understand the first thing about love," she whispered.

"*You're* the one who's trying to hurt *me!*" he yelled.

She turned away, blinking rapidly to hold back the tears that threatened to spill from her eyes. Her gaze rested on the computer, and she thought of all their e-mail messages and chat-room dates. Freeverse and Quarter would never say such terrible things to each other. Why couldn't real life be so simple?

"I never meant to hurt you," she said slowly, the words rough in her throat. She swallowed and continued in a clear voice. "But you want something you have no right to demand of me."

"If that's how you feel about it, then we're through," Ken said. He sat down at the computer, fixing his eyes on the monitor as if he was alone in the room.

Olivia watched him for a minute in silence, her heart breaking at the thought of all they had lost. Then she nodded and walked out the door.

Chapter 8

Jessica finally caught up with Lila and Amy as they emerged from the cafeteria line at noon on Monday. "Hey, guys!" she called over the cheerful lunchtime din. "Glad you could put in a cameo. Where were you all morning? I've been trying to find you so we could talk about the party!"

"Shhh!" Lila cautioned, nodding toward the table across the room where Elizabeth, Enid, Maria Slater, and Olivia were sitting down to lunch. "It's not safe to discuss it in the cafeteria. Maybe we should talk after school instead."

Jessica cocked an eyebrow at her. "I think we're OK here," she said, "unless my sister has suddenly developed bionic hearing."

Amy and Lila exchanged an unreadable

glance. "You can't be too careful," Amy said.

"All right, then let's eat in the courtyard," Jessica said, ushering them toward the door. "We can finalize the plans while we work on our tans."

"The Plan?" Amy squeaked.

"The *plans*," Jessica repeated. "What's your deal?"

Amy bit her lip, and Lila smiled brightly.

"Nothing!" Lila said.

"All morning every time I've spotted one of you in the hall, you've disappeared before I could catch up," Jessica said, narrowing her eyes. "In English class you both popped in right when the bell rang and dematerialized as soon as Mr. Collins set us free."

"Sorry, Jess," Amy replied as they headed toward their favorite sunny spot. "You know how things get around exam time."

Lila rolled her eyes, and Jessica hooted with laughter.

"As if!" Jessica exclaimed. "Finals don't start for a whole week. Amy Sutton, you have never in your life studied for a test that early."

"Then I guess I've been swamped with other things all morning," Amy said quickly.

Lila settled down on the grass and pulled out her monogrammed canvas lunch bag. "Well, *I* tried to find *you* this morning, but I couldn't," she told Jessica. "Do you have my money yet, Wakefield?"

"I *told* you I'd get it to you when I see Steven," Jessica said. "Back off a little." Jessica leaned against a tree and stared glumly at her hamburger, wishing she'd taken the time to make herself lunch that morning. "Is this a hamburger or a hockey puck? At least the french fries are edible," she added after sampling one. "But we have more important things to worry about. Let's talk about the party on Friday!"

Amy was stealing a french fry from Jessica's tray, but her hand froze in midair. "I wouldn't worry about the party, Jess," she replied. "It seems to me like we have it under control."

Lila nodded enthusiastically. "Sure, we do," she agreed, lifting a plastic container of sushi from her bag. "I already rented the tent and hired the musicians, and the invitations are out. What more is there to do?"

"Oh, just planning, buying, and putting together every bit of the food and decorations," Jessica informed her. "It's a ton of work!"

"You're overreacting as usual," Lila told her. "Besides, you don't have any money." Lila cast a glance at Amy, and Amy hid a giggle behind her hand.

Jessica thought she was going to scream. She took a long sip from her carton of chocolate milk, trying to calm herself, but when she spoke, her voice rose in frustration. "So the tent place wouldn't take my mom's credit card! So what? I've used it dozens of times."

"Then go out and buy a little food. What's the big deal?" Lila asked.

"I can't believe I have to tell you this, Li! You of all people know how much work it takes. You've planned more parties than everyone else in town put together!"

"Somebody's inner child is feeling cranky today," Amy said. Jessica glared at her. She hated it when Amy started using the psychological lingo she'd picked up while working at the Project Youth crisis hot line.

"I thought you were both going to help me!" Jessica exclaimed.

Lila stared down her nose at Jessica. "Honestly, what do I look like, Physical Labor Girl? I'm a concept person and, apparently, a free money machine. Actually doing work is *your* department."

"First of all, *I'm going to pay you back!* And second, the party was *my* idea, Ms. Concept Person," Jessica insisted. "Third, you promised you'd help!"

"I am helping you," Lila reminded her. "On top of everything else I let you put my cell phone number on your invitations. I can't do everything."

"Oh, I almost forgot to ask! How many RSVPs have you gotten?"

Lila shrugged. "A bunch."

"A bunch? After eleven years of math classes that's the best you can do?"

"It's not like she memorized the RSVP list," Amy said.

"The list is in my locker," Lila said. "I'll check it when I get a chance, and I'll let you know exactly how many have called. But don't worry, lots of people will be there."

"How can I not worry when my two best friends are suddenly too busy to help me?" Jessica demanded.

Lila breathed a long, pained sigh. "All right," she agreed. "I'll help you put up decorations and set out the food on Friday."

"But I need help *now!*" Jessica cried, mystified by her friends' attitude reversal.

"It's not like we don't have a life outside your sister's birthday," Amy reminded her.

Jessica turned back to Lila. "Look, if you're worried about who gets the credit, then forget everything I said about coming up with the party theme myself. You can take all the credit for the idea."

Lila smiled smugly. "It's about time I got some recognition for my excellent efforts."

"So now will you help me?" Jessica asked hopefully.

"Get real," Lila said, flicking her hair off her shoulder.

Jessica stared at her for a moment, eyes wide. Then she turned back to Amy, who was in the process of swiping another french fry from Jessica's lunch. "Amy, *you'll* come party shopping with me after school today, won't you?"

"Sorry, Jessica. I was planning to give myself a manicure this afternoon."

"A manicure?" Jessica asked. "Your cuticles are more important than my birthday party?"

Amy shrugged. "It's not *your* birthday party exactly," she reminded her. "It's your nerdy sister's."

"So? What difference does that make? I'm hosting it!"

"You'll do fine buying party stuff without us," Lila said. "If there's one thing I've taught you over the years, it's how to shop."

"But you know I need one of you to drive me. My parents both took their cars to work today!"

"There's a public bus that goes downtown from our neighborhood," Amy reminded her. Amy also lived on Calico Drive, four blocks from the Wakefields.

Jessica couldn't believe her ears. "You would let me lug packages around on a smelly old bus rather than go shopping with me?"

"You've ridden the bus before," Amy remarked. "And it didn't kill you."

"OK, so how about a shopping trip tomorrow? Or Wednesday?"

"We can't do it Wednesday. There's that meeting," Amy said. Her voice choked on the last word, and Jessica noticed that Lila cast her a thunderous glare.

"What meeting?" Jessica asked. "What kind of meeting would you two be going to that I don't know about?"

"Project Youth," Amy said quickly. "It's about a new program we're starting up. It's a, uh, support group for children in single-parent households."

Jessica stared at Lila. "Since when are *you* involved in do-gooder projects? Do you have any idea what a little altruism could do to your reputation?"

Lila gave Amy a sidelong glance. "It's not like I'm actually *working* for Project Youth," she said. "My parents donated some of the money for this program. Mom couldn't make it on Wednesday, so she asked me to go in her place."

Jessica didn't believe it for an instant. Her friends were definitely hiding something. Suddenly she grinned, realizing exactly what was going on: *They must be planning a birthday present for me!* It was the only explanation.

"OK, forget Wednesday. Your meeting is more important. Any objections to tomorrow?"

"We both have dates," Lila said quickly.

"This is so typical!" Jessica cried. "You two never want to do any actual work!"

Amy nodded solemnly. "Your point being?"

"The point is that I need your help!" Jessica said. "What happened to all the shopping advice you promised me?"

Lila smiled. "Listen carefully," she said. "Here's your shopping advice from a pro: Don't spend too much money!" Her face turned serious. "I really mean that, Jessica. Don't go overboard spending money on this thing, or you'll regret it later."

Elizabeth unwrapped her tuna sandwich and looked up at her friends. "So what's next on our party-planning list?" she asked Enid, Olivia, and Maria Slater, who were sitting with her in the school cafeteria on Monday. "Shopping was a bust this weekend, so I guess we need to schedule another trip. Can you two make it this afternoon?"

"I'm sorry, Liz," Maria told her. "But Mr. Jaworski's history exam is supposed to be a major bummer. I was planning to hit the books again after school today."

"Olivia?" Elizabeth asked hopefully.

"I'm, uh, going over to Maria's so we can study together."

"Looks like it's you and me, Enid," Elizabeth said. "You've got your mom's hatchback. Can we go straight from school?"

Enid shook her head. "I wish I could, Liz. But my mother gets off work early today. She needs her car by four o'clock."

"Then we'll go later tonight. You said you'd handle the decorations. You can look at crepe paper and stuff while I pick up some things in the snacks section."

Enid swallowed. "I, um, have to study later tonight."

Elizabeth sighed. "Let me guess: Mr. Jaworski's history final."

"I'm way worried about it," Enid said.

"I'm surprised the three of you are putting in so much time on that exam. You're all good at history, and Mr. Jaworski said it shouldn't be difficult for students who've kept up all semester."

"It's the dates!" Olivia said quickly, and Maria and Enid nodded their agreement. "It's so easy to freeze up and forget exactly when everything happened."

"Don't worry about the decorations, Liz," Enid said. "I promise I'll take care of everything that needs to be done. Let me surprise you with them."

"I'll help her," Olivia added. "Just leave it to us."

Elizabeth had always trusted her friends completely, but now she had an unfamiliar, uncertain feeling about their assurances. She nodded reluctantly. "That's great, but I'm still worried about the munchies. I really need some input from all of you."

"We still have time," Maria said reassuringly. "You need to mellow out. We'll pull it together by the end of the week."

"Then let's do a shopping trip tomorrow."

Olivia shook her head. "I can't. I've got to talk with Ms. Markey about my entry in the art show."

"Are you entering Ken's portrait?" Maria asked.

"I might as well now that I've broken up with him over it."

"Broken up?" Enid asked. "You and Ken? For good?"

"Olivia, I'm sorry," Elizabeth said, momentarily distracted from her own problems. If Olivia was acting a little strangely, she certainly had cause, Elizabeth realized. *And I've been too wrapped up in my party planning to show her much sympathy.* "I didn't know."

"Let's not talk about it," Olivia said. "I'm trying to keep my mind on anything else—even schoolwork."

"I can give you plenty to think about if you want to focus on pretzels and diet soda," Elizabeth said. "How about coming shopping with me Wednesday?"

"I have a meeting," Olivia said quickly. Then she blushed bright pink.

"What kind of meeting?" Elizabeth asked, curious.

"It's, uh, for the *Oracle*, to discuss the graduation issue."

"Are you sure you've got the date right?" Elizabeth asked. "I didn't hear about any *Oracle* meeting on Wednesday, and I'm sure Penny would have let me know if there was one." Penny Ayala, a senior, was the editor in chief of the school newspaper.

"That's because *I* called this meeting. It's just for my arts staff," said Olivia, arts editor for the *Oracle*. But she was blushing as she said it, and Elizabeth wondered if she was hiding something.

Elizabeth turned to Maria and Enid. "Can either of you two do a shopping trip on Wednesday?"

"I'll be at Olivia's meeting," Maria said, flustered. "I, uh, told her I'd write an article." Unlike Elizabeth and Olivia, Maria wasn't officially on the *Oracle* staff, but she did write an occasional article as a freelancer.

"And I'm meeting with Mr. Russo about some makeup work in chemistry," Enid said.

"Can you spare any time after your chat with Mr. Russo?" Elizabeth asked her.

"I have to study."

Elizabeth was getting seriously frustrated. "What if everyone else is as busy studying for finals as you three?" Elizabeth asked, biting her lip. "What if nobody can come? Why does our birthday have to fall just before exams?"

"Girlfriend, you need to chill," Maria told her. "If you plan it, they will come. I know they will."

"Enid, have you gotten any RSVPs?" Elizabeth asked.

"I, uh, don't know an exact number," Enid said. "I haven't counted up the names. But almost everyone has called to say yes. There's no reason to be uptight about it."

"No reason?" Elizabeth's eyes widened as she stared at Enid. "You know Mel is going to hike up the price beyond my limit if I don't get a hundred people there. How can you be so calm about it?"

Enid just blinked, then looked down at her lunch.

"You are seriously losing it, girl," Maria said, placing a hand on Elizabeth's arm. "I'm sure everyone will be primed for a party by Friday."

"And what if they are?" Elizabeth asked, turning to Maria. "I won't be ready! I'm planning a major surprise party for four days from now, and suddenly nobody wants to help me with the preparations!" Her three friends looked at one another uncomfortably, and Elizabeth figured they must be feeling guilty. Suddenly she felt guilty too. Maybe she was expecting too much of them. She took a deep breath to steady her nerves.

"We're sorry, Elizabeth," Enid said, her fair skin blushing pink. "We don't mean to abandon you in the

117

middle of the planning, but we're kind of worried about finals."

Elizabeth nodded. "I'm sorry too. I don't mean to freak out. I wouldn't expect you to jeopardize your grades. It's just that I want this to be a party Jessica will remember forever."

"It will be, Liz," Olivia assured her. "I have a feeling it's going to be more memorable than anything you or Jessica can imagine."

"You can count on me for Friday afternoon," Enid promised. "I'll spend as much time as you need setting things up at the Beach Disco and picking up any last minute items. Mom already said I could have the car that day."

"Thanks, Enid," Elizabeth said. She was grateful for her friend's promise, but she had a sinking feeling that Enid's help on Friday afternoon wouldn't be nearly enough.

Seniors had to stay after school on Tuesday to order their caps and gowns for graduation, so Bruce didn't arrive home until the family was sitting down to dinner in the mansion's formal dining room.

"Where the heck is today's mail?" he cried, racing into the candlelit dining room. He was still waiting for his letter from Harvard, and time was running out. Penny had been rejected days ago. Was it even possible that he could still be accepted? "There's nothing for me on the table in the front hall."

"You do have one letter," his father announced with a broad smile. "I brought it in here so you could open it before we eat."

Henry Patman held out a letter-size envelope with a Harvard Admissions Office imprint. Bruce gulped. It was a regular, business-size envelope. Everyone knew rejection letters came in small envelopes. Acceptances came in large packets, with course booklets, campus maps, and dormitory applications. Bruce himself already had tons of experience with flat, letter-size envelopes.

"Is something wrong, Bruce?" his mother asked as he gingerly took the envelope and sat down, turning it over and over in his hands.

"Not a thing," Bruce said breezily, avoiding the eyes of his cousin, Roger Barrett Patman, who lived with Bruce's family and was seated across the table from him. Unlike Mr. and Mrs. Patman, Roger would know what a little envelope was supposed to mean. Bruce shook his head as if that could clear the anxiety from it. Surely a rule like that didn't apply to every school, he told himself. Everyone knew Harvard was in a class by itself. This letter must be his acceptance. The dormitory and class information would arrive in a few days.

"Aren't you going to open it, son?" his father asked sharply as Miranda and Dwight began serving the soup.

Bruce nodded, convinced he was right. He had to be. He used his butter knife to carefully slit open the envelope, then slowly withdrew the letter.

"'Dear Applicant,'" he read aloud, his mouth going completely dry at the impersonal salutation. He drained his crystal water goblet before continuing. "'Thank you for your interest in Harvard University and your patience with our waiting-list procedures. We regret that we cannot offer you admission at this time. The incoming freshman class has now been filled. . . .'"

Bruce's voice trailed off as his entire body went numb.

His mother reached over to pat his hand, but Bruce could hardly feel her fingers. "I'm sorry, honey," she said. "I know how much you wanted to go there."

Mr. Patman's face was less sympathetic. "What schools haven't you heard from?"

Bruce shook his head weakly. "I've heard from all of them, Dad," he choked out. "I didn't get in anywhere."

"Didn't you apply to a safety school, like California State?" Roger asked.

Bruce fought the urge to throw his bowl of soup at his cousin. "I didn't bother," he revealed, his voice wavering as he twisted the hem of the white linen tablecloth in his fingers. "I thought I'd get into Harvard. I—"

"So what does that mean for your future?" Mr. Patman stared at him, jaw clenched, as if Bruce were a cockroach on the chateaubriand platter.

I have no future, Bruce wanted to say. *My life is over.* "I don't know," he whispered instead, terrified that he was about to fall to pieces in front of his father. "May I be excused, please?"

"No, you may not, Bruce," his father said sternly. "*We* have to talk about this."

"I can't right now, all right?" Bruce blurted as he stood. He was dangerously close to cracking up, and he had to get out of the suffocating room now. He turned and strode quickly through the side door.

"This conversation isn't over, son," his father called after him. "Not by a long shot."

"The Plan is going full speed ahead," Lila announced to the group of Jessica and Elizabeth's friends who were gathered around her swimming pool Wednesday afternoon. It seemed odd to Lila, having people like Enid Rollins sitting there at Fowler Crest with her own more socially acceptable friends. But she supposed Jessica was worth some minor contact with the nerdish element.

"Enid, did you fix the Beach Disco?" Maria

Santelli asked, tapping her clipboard with a pen.

Enid nodded. "It's all taken care of." She laughed, holding up her crossed fingers. "The manager, Mel, and I are just like this."

"Mel has a major crush on her!" Maria Slater added.

Lila rolled her eyes as she accepted a glass of mineral water from a maid who was bustling by, carrying a tray of soft drinks. Fat, fortyish Mel was about as good as geeky Enid could hope for.

"Elizabeth will freak when she arrives at the Beach Disco on Friday to set up!" Olivia said.

"She'll get over it," Amy said with a shrug.

Jade turned to Lila. "What about the musicians?"

"They were putty in my hands," Lila bragged. "Of course, most people are."

Maria consulted her clipboard again. "Decorations?"

"Enid and I have them covered," Olivia said.

"Don't cover them *too* well," the other Maria joked, helping herself to some nachos. "Isn't that the whole idea of decorations—to let people see them?"

Lila groaned. "I thought we decided to keep Egbert out of this so we could be spared the lame jokes."

Maria Santelli sighed, her fingers tightening on her pen. "Winston's out of it because he's got the biggest mouth in California."

"Haven't you two made up yet?" Annie asked her.

"No, and we're not likely to," Maria said. "At least not in this century."

"Your little love squabbles are fascinating," Lila pointed out. "But we do have more urgent matters to discuss."

"Are the twins' parents on board?" Aaron asked.

"*On* board?" Lila exclaimed. "I've talked to the Parental Ones, and believe me, Ned and Alice are going way *overboard!* Wait until you see! But don't worry. They're definitely with us. And so is a certain Wakefield brother."

"Steven's with *you,* at least," Aaron said with a smirk.

Lila stared down her nose at him.

"Oh, no! Not *The Look!*" Aaron cried, raising his arms as if to ward off an attack.

Not long before, Lila had dated Steven Wakefield—to both twins' horror—when he was home from Sweet Valley University to intern with the local district attorney's office. The relationship had been a mistake all around, Lila knew now. She and Steven had absolutely nothing in common. They'd come together only because a fire had devastated part of her family's mansion and Lila had been blamed for it—until Steven helped clear her name.

Afterward Lila had been happy to hear that Steven and his girlfriend Billie Winkler were back together again. And she had no desire to relive any part of the whole weird episode—either the part about dating Steven or the part about being a suspected arsonist.

"For your information, Mr. and Mrs. Wakefield called Steven, not me," Lila said coldly to Aaron. "But he and that Billie person are both part of The Plan now."

Maria Slater dipped a bare foot in the sparkling water of the Fowlers' swimming pool. "It sounds like The Plan is going along, uh, *swimmingly*," she said with a grin.

Lila rolled her eyes, although secretly she was glad for Maria's help in steering the subject away from Steven. "Thank you, *Winston*, for another hokey attempt at humor," she said dryly.

Maria Santelli pointed at Lila and Enid with her pen. "What are you telling Jessica and Elizabeth about the RSVPs?"

"Jess asked me the other day, and I totally froze," Lila admitted. "I made up something about having left the list in my locker, but sooner or later she's going to ask again. What should I say?"

"Lie to her," Enid directed.

"You certainly chose the right person for the job," Maria Slater remarked. Lila glared.

"Well, sort of lie," Enid continued. "Tell Jess

that everyone has been calling to say they'll be at her party. That's what I told Liz when she asked."

"Good," Maria Santelli said, pushing back her long dark hair. "Each twin has to believe that her shindig is going ahead exactly as she's planned it."

"Elizabeth is becoming a basket case over the way we keep avoiding helping with the planning," Olivia said. "We couldn't stop her from buying the snacks herself. She thinks we've all abandoned her."

"There's no way to help it," Annie pointed out, "unless we tell her the truth about The Plan."

"And that is so out of the question," Aaron concluded.

"Personally, I kind of like watching Jessica squirm," Lila admitted. "She's entertaining when she's wigging out."

Maria Santelli laughed. "It's only two more days. After that we'll blow them both away with what happens on Friday night."

"We certainly will," Lila agreed. "Jessica and Elizabeth wanted to surprise each other on their birthday. Now, thanks to us, they'll *both* be surprised!"

Chapter 9

Jessica skipped into Elizabeth's room early on the morning of their birthday. Prince Albert raced behind her, barking skittishly. "Wake up, Lizzie! Wake up!" Jessica called. "Hey, doggie!" she said, petting his soft golden back. "You're as excited as I am about today, aren't you?"

Prince Albert nudged Elizabeth with his nose, and she opened one eye groggily. "Why are you both here? My alarm doesn't even go off for another half hour!"

"Who needs an alarm? Come on, Lizzie. Time to rise and shine!"

"Don't we have this backward?" Elizabeth asked, sitting up and blinking. "*I'm* supposed to be the one who gets *you* out of bed."

"Not today!" Jessica cried, pulling the comforter off her sister's pajama-clad form. "You don't want to miss a single minute of our first day of being seventeen, do you?"

Elizabeth's eyes snapped open. "Seventeen!" she repeated incredulously, her mouth widening into a grin. "We're seventeen years old. That is totally cool, even if it is the middle of the night."

"Happy birthday to us!" Jessica sang out. Prince Albert barked along frantically, as if adding his own birthday greeting.

"You might want to crank up the volume a little, Jessica. Someone in San Diego didn't hear you."

"Spoilsport!" Jessica complained gleefully.

Elizabeth swung her legs over the side of the bed. "As long as we're awake at the crack of dawn, we might as well get dressed."

An hour later the twins hurried downstairs together and followed the scent of warm cinnamon into the kitchen. Jessica grinned broadly when she saw who was seated at the table with her parents.

"Steven and Billie!" she screamed, throwing her arms around her brother. With his six-foot-one frame, dark brown hair, and chocolate-colored eyes, Steven looked exactly like an eighteen-year-old version of his father.

"I didn't know you were coming!" Elizabeth

said, giving Steven's girlfriend a hug and then reaching around Jessica to peck her brother on the cheek. "Either of you. Why didn't you tell me when I talked to you on the phone last weekend?"

"Because we all wanted it to be a surprise," Mrs. Wakefield told them as she poured glasses of cranberry juice. Jessica noticed her mother and Steven glance quickly at each other and then look away. "Happy birthday, girls!"

"We got up early, threw our junk in the Volkswagen, and figured on being here in time for breakfast," Billie said.

"It's French toast," Mr. Wakefield said, stepping aside so they could see the electric griddle on the counter. "Your favorite!" Prince Albert nudged him urgently, but Mr. Wakefield swatted him away. "What's with this schizo dog today?" he asked good-naturedly. "I've never seen him so keyed up."

"He's happy because we're seventeen years old!" Jessica sang out. Prince Albert howled along with her.

Steven pointed at Jessica and the golden retriever. "I'm not sure which one of them has the worse singing voice!"

"Can you stay all weekend?" Elizabeth asked him, raising her voice to be heard above the mayhem.

"Absolutely," Steven promised. "Neither of us has another exam until Tuesday. We'll have to hit the books at some point, but you're stuck with us until then!"

Prince Albert began running circles around the table. "How can you possibly study in all this?" Elizabeth asked, gesturing around the room with a laugh.

Her mother placed a bowl of cut strawberries on the table. "It's just another quiet, subdued breakfast with the Wakefield family!"

"That's all right," Billie said. "My exam Tuesday is on chaos theory."

"Glad we could help," Elizabeth replied.

Jessica settled herself on her brother's lap, knowing she was acting as if it were her seventh birthday instead of her seventeenth but not caring in the least. "So, big brother, did you bring me a present?"

"There's nothing like the direct approach," Steven remarked.

"That's our Jessica," Mr. Wakefield said. He lifted the first slice of French toast from the griddle. "The first two pieces are for the birthday girls."

"I can't eat until I see my present from Steven and Billie!" Jessica protested.

"Arghh!" Steven complained. "If you have to sit on my lap, Jess, please don't bounce. I think you just gave me an appendectomy."

"You should thank me. Think of how much you'd have had to pay a surgeon for that!"

Billie pulled two identical packages from Steven's backpack, wrapped in the Sunday comics. "Excuse the elegant wrapping job," she said, handing one small, flat package to each twin. "We have to keep up our image as poor, struggling students."

"Thank you, guys," Elizabeth said. "But having you here on our birthday is more than enough. You didn't have to get us anything!"

"Sure, they did!" Jessica argued.

"I'll remember that this summer on my nineteenth birthday!" Steven told her.

Jessica shook the package near her ear for effect, though it was obvious from its size and shape that the gift was a CD. "Hmmm . . . it's too small to be a new car."

"It's the inflatable kind," Billie explained with a grin.

Jessica climbed off Steven's lap and sat in her own chair as her father reached across Prince Albert to set a plate of cinnamon-speckled French toast in front of her. The dog nearly knocked him over.

"OK, Liz," Jessica began, "we open them together. On your mark, get ready . . . unwrap!"

Jessica tore frantically through the paper, ripping the box open while Elizabeth was still slitting the wrapping on her own package with a butter knife.

"Jamie Peters's new CD!" Jessica squealed. Prince Albert barked his approval. "Even Lila doesn't have this one yet," Jessica added. "Thank you! I love it!"

Elizabeth carefully unfolded the paper from around hers. "Colleen Dunstan!" she exclaimed with a pleased smile. "Olivia played this for me the other day, and it's got some terrific songs on it. Thanks, guys." She kissed both Steven and Billie on the cheek.

Jessica rolled her eyes. "Colleen Dunstan? The one who sings about bombings and famines? Now *there's* a singer who knows how to party down!"

"Some of the best music in the history of rock has been about social protest," Mrs. Wakefield reminded her.

"I forget that our parents are former flower children," Jessica said. "That is so embarrassing!"

"Jessica!" Elizabeth exclaimed.

"Seventeen," Mr. Wakefield mused. "That's one of those ages when kids are *supposed* to be embarrassed by their parents, right?"

"So Jessica is just fulfilling the role society has cast her in," Steven concluded.

"Somebody's been taking sociology this semester," his mother remarked.

Prince Albert was pawing at the back door, barking wildly. "That dog is totally manic!" Steven said, rising to open the door. The dog rushed out and began running laps around the backyard. "What have you been feeding him since last time I was home? Mexican jumping beans? Espresso-flavored dog biscuits?"

Jessica felt a twinge of guilt. "I guess I haven't taken him out for exercise nearly enough this week. I've been too busy planning the—" She stopped, resisting the urge to clap a hand over her mouth. She had just about spilled the beans about Elizabeth's party. "Planning for, um, exams and summer vacation," she completed quickly.

"I've been too busy too," Elizabeth said. "He'll be fine if we let him run around the backyard until we get home this afternoon."

"Well, there's still twenty minutes before Lila's coming by to pick me up for school," Jessica pointed out. "That's enough time to open another present, if anyone has any that should be opened. . . ."

"Subtle, Jessica. Very subtle," Elizabeth said.

"I don't have any presents," their mother said. "Do you have any, Ned?"

"No, I'm fresh out of presents," he replied.

Jessica nodded knowingly. "I get it. The parental presents aren't happening until tonight. That's cruel, Mom and Dad. You're going to feel really guilty if I die of curiosity between now and then."

"We'll risk it," said Mrs. Wakefield.

"Uh, Jessica, I was planning to give you my present tonight as well," Elizabeth told her.

"I'm glad to hear you say that because that's exactly what I was going to do," Jessica said with a sigh, hoping desperately that she could come up with a present by then.

Not to mention an entire party, she reminded herself. Her friends had deserted her this week when it came to getting things ready for it. Now time was almost up. If Lila backed out on her offer to help this afternoon, Elizabeth's birthday would be a total disaster.

Devon sat in chemistry class on Friday morning, staring across the room at Elizabeth instead of listening to Mr. Russo's review of material that would be on next week's exam. Devon wasn't a model student like Elizabeth. Most of the time he just couldn't get motivated to care about the periodic table or the definition of an acid. But he had a quick mind and a phenomenal memory. Good grades came easily.

Right now, he realized, the only chemistry he could think about was the chemistry that seemed to electrify the air between himself and Elizabeth. Unfortunately, she seemed totally oblivious to it. He'd certainly done his best lately not to let her know how he felt. After their stiff, impersonal conversation in front of the post office he'd decided that they were going to just be friends, and he planned to stick by that decision.

"Mr. Whitelaw!" A loud voice broke into his thoughts. "If you'd care to join us on this planet—"

"Sorry, Mr. Russo," he replied. "What was the question?"

"Name three of the properties of a base, Mr. Whitelaw," the teacher repeated in a weary voice.

"Soluble in water, pH greater than 7, and can react with an acid to form a salt," he replied automatically.

Mr. Russo stared at him for a moment before reluctantly admitting, "Correct. Now, Miss Wakefield, how does an acid differ from a base?"

Devon turned back to gaze at Elizabeth as she

answered the question flawlessly. She was so lovely, with her blond hair and blue-green eyes. But it was a lot more than looks. Plenty of girls were pretty. Even Jessica, technically Elizabeth's mirror image, never looked as beautiful to him as her twin did. Elizabeth had a natural openness and honesty that seemed to shine through her face. Except that he wasn't supposed to notice that anymore. They were just friends.

Now it was Elizabeth's seventeenth birthday, and he hadn't the faintest idea what gift he was going to give her. Looking at the way the sunlight from the window traced gold highlights in her hair, he longed to buy her an armful of roses and a ring that would show the world how he felt.

But I don't feel that way anymore, he reminded himself as Mr. Russo moved on to his next victim. *I feel like her friend. That's all!* If only it were true. But he needed to think of a gift that was right to give to a friend—not even a very close friend, he decided. A gift that would signify nothing more than friendship. He didn't want Elizabeth to think he was pathetically pining for her. He had only a few hours to think up a gift that would prove to Elizabeth, once and for all, that he wasn't still hung up on her.

Chapter 10

"I am so psyched about tonight!" Elizabeth exclaimed as Enid drove the blue hatchback out of the parking lot of Sweet Valley High that afternoon. Despite her recent problems with Todd and Devon, Elizabeth couldn't remember the last time she'd been this happy. She was seventeen years old, her family was home together for the weekend, and she felt closer to her friends than ever—even if they were studying too hard to help much with the birthday celebration.

"Does Jessica know anything about the party?" Enid asked, fiddling with the knob on the radio.

"She doesn't have a clue. She's going to be so surprised!"

"She's not the only one."

Elizabeth glanced at her strangely. "What do you mean?"

"Just that, uh, Jessica's friends are going to be blown away too," Enid told her after she'd settled on a light rock station. "I mean, people like Lila and Amy always assume that people like you and me couldn't plan a wild and crazy party if our lives depended on it. I bet they're expecting this to be lame."

Elizabeth giggled. Enid must be excited too. She was chattering at about twice the normal speed. "You're right," Elizabeth replied. "They're in for a shock. This is going to be the best birthday bash ever!"

"Did you ever come up with a gift for Jessica?" Enid asked.

"That's the one thing I'm bummed about," Elizabeth admitted. "I've been so busy putting this party together that I haven't had time to deal with a present for her." She might have found the time, she thought, if her friends had given her the help she'd expected on the party planning. But it was no use worrying about that now.

"Enid! Watch out!" Elizabeth cried as something darted into the street in front of them. The car swerved wildly, and the curb rushed at Elizabeth as the world seemed to blur around her.

Then the squirrel disappeared through a hedge, and the car straightened to resume its progress. "Wow, a kamikaze squirrel!" Enid said a moment later, still breathing heavily.

"That was close," Elizabeth replied, her heart pounding. "I never knew you were so good at evasive maneuvers! If we were surfers, I'd call that a *gnarly* display of driving."

"Gnarly? Is that good?"

"It's awesome!"

"I have to confess, Liz, the whole thing was planned. Psycho Squirrel and I conspired together to come up with some extra excitement for your birthday."

"I'm betting the conspiracy is bigger than that," Elizabeth joked. "Are you sure you didn't send Prince Albert an e-mail about it as well? He was Crazy Dog all morning, rushing around like a fur-covered tornado!"

"I didn't know dogs got caught up in the birthday spirit."

"He was almost as bad as Jessica!" Elizabeth said with a chuckle. "She was totally manic. Our wild and crazy party tonight will suit her mood perfectly!"

"A wild and crazy party deserves wild and crazy music," Enid said, reaching again for the radio. "We need something to get us in a party mood!"

A moment later an old John Mellencamp song blared out of the speakers, and both girls sang along loudly—off-key, in Elizabeth's case. *"When the walls come tumbling down . . ."*

"That's more like it!" Elizabeth called over the music. "The music tonight is going to be just as loud, the way Jessica likes it. Dana promised me that the Droids would blow the roof off the place!"

Enid steered into the parking lot of the Beach Disco. From where they sat, the ocean waves seemed unusually high. But the sky was clear, with no sign of a storm.

"That's weird," Elizabeth said, gazing out the window at the sky. "I don't think there's a single seagull around. This part of the coast is usually full of them. It seems so quiet."

"Quiet? Are you kidding? Those waves could drown out the Droids!"

"But I'm used to hearing those eerie little cries that the gulls make. Now I don't hear any at all. I wonder where they've gone."

"Probably at home putting on their snazziest feathers so they can celebrate your birthday in style," Enid said. Her words were glib, but her voice sounded tense. Elizabeth felt a pang of guilt. Obviously the stress of party planning was affecting Enid nearly as much as it affected Elizabeth.

Elizabeth jumped out of the car into the still, salt-scented air. Her friend remained in the driver's seat. "Is something wrong, Enid?"

Enid took a deep breath. "No, everything's fine," she said. "Let's go face the moment of truth."

"That's a weird thing to say about decorating for a party," Elizabeth told her.

Enid laughed weakly. "I guess I'm just nervous about everything going according to plan."

"I cannot believe I'm playing chauffeur again," Lila complained, gunning the engine of her classic lime green Triumph and shooting out of the school parking lot. "If it were for anyone else, Jess, and any other day of the year . . ."

"Don't worry," Jessica assured her from the passenger seat. "Your secret life as a commoner is safe with me."

"On to the beach? Or do you have other menial tasks you want me to perform first?"

"There are plenty more menial tasks to come," Jessica promised, "but they're all on the beach."

"It's a good thing the shop agreed to deliver the tent there," Lila remarked. "We'd never fit it in a sports car. As long as we're meeting them there to get it from them, couldn't you ask them to set it up for us too?"

"If my name were Rockefeller or Du Pont or Fowler, I probably could. But it's not, so it's just you and me, kid. Unless you hid a few of your servants in the trunk?"

"No such luck," Lila admitted.

"It reeks that Amy wimped out on us! Do you know how hard it's going to be to erect that tent with only two people?"

"Oh, boy, manual labor. I can't wait."

"She said she had a date with Barry this afternoon," Jessica complained. "She thinks she's all that, planning a date on my birthday. It's not like she won't see him tonight at my party!"

"At least somebody still has a love life," Lila said. "I mean, how many people have you heard of lately going on a serious date? In the last month it seems like every couple at school has flat lined."

"Yeah, did you hear about Ken and Olivia? Amy says she painted some nudie portrait of him. I wouldn't mind getting a look at that picture! But I can't blame him for being mad."

"Or for dropping her on the basis of weirdness alone," Lila said with an ungracious sniff. "What did a stud like Ken ever see in that flaked-out artist?"

"Totally incompatible," Jessica agreed.

"And then there's Winston and Maria. . . ."

Jessica shook her head. "If you ask me, she should have dumped that Nightmare on Nerd Street long ago!"

"The breakups are all your sister's fault, you know. She blew it with Todd and Devon, and romance at Sweet Valley High has been downhill ever since!"

An hour later the two girls were on the beach, struggling with the huge party tent. The tide was higher than normal, so they were trying to set up the tent on a bluff overlooking the ocean, where its canvas folds kept catching the wind. Every time one part of the tent seemed stable, another part would collapse. Jessica lost track of the number of times she'd been pummeled by a heavy sheet of canvas. And she'd never seen Lila so sweaty.

"Hey, Li!" she called suddenly, frantically smoothing back her hair. "Hunk alert down the beach. Check it out!"

Two tall, well-built guys in bathing trunks and sweatshirts were strolling toward them, a thin layer of surf stretching around their ankles with every incoming wave.

"The blond-haired one is mine," Jessica whispered. "Hands off!"

"Fine with me. The dark-haired one's taller!" Lila replied.

"Act helpless," Jessica advised. "We'll have them putting up this tent for us in no time!"

As the two guys approached, Jessica saw that they were probably in their midtwenties and that both had terrific suntans. She could have sworn she saw the dark-haired one wink at Lila. *That could be useful,* she thought. *If Mr. Tall, Dark, and Handsome wants to impress Lila, he'll be thrilled at the chance to help us.*

"Hello, girls," said the blond. "What in the world are you doing?"

Jessica smiled her most dazzling smile, batting her eyelashes and wishing she were wearing a bikini instead of biker shorts and an oversize T-shirt. "We're just trying to put up this nasty old tent for my birthday party tonight. But I'm afraid it's going to take someone a lot stronger than us!"

"Well, happy birthday," he responded, his eyes twinkling in the sunlight of late afternoon. "How big a party is this going to be?"

Jessica turned her head slightly so he could get the full effect of the sunshine in her hair. "Why don't you two plan to stop by in a few hours, and you can see for yourself?"

"If it's more than ten people—," the dark-haired man began, his eyes on Lila.

Lila interrupted him, laughing. "Well, of

course! It's way more than ten people. What kind of a birthday party would it be with only ten people?"

"Then I'm afraid we're going to have to see your permit," the blond man informed them.

Something small and hard plummeted, burning, from Jessica's throat to the pit of her stomach. "What permit?" she squeaked out.

"We're with the Beach Patrol," the light-haired guy explained. "And you're required to have a permit in order to hold a party on the beach."

"We, uh, forgot where we left the permit!" Jessica lied. "I'll find it by tomorrow, and I'll bring it to you then."

"I'm sorry," said the dark-haired man. "But we have to see it now, before your guests arrive. That's the rule."

"If we can't find it, can you just issue me a new one?" Jessica tried, desperate.

He checked his watch. "Sorry, but the office is already closed for the weekend."

"What if we can't show you a permit?" Jessica asked, dreading the answer.

"Then I'm afraid this party is over before it gets started."

Chapter 11

Enid's heart was pounding as she walked with Elizabeth into Mel's office. "We're here to set up for the Wakefield party tonight," Elizabeth told him.

Mel gave Enid a lingering glance, and she silently urged him to be more discreet. Enid could see that Elizabeth had noticed the look, but from her knowing grin it was clear she'd misinterpreted it. Enid didn't care what Elizabeth thought was going through Mel's mind as long as she remained in the dark about Enid's role in what was about to happen. It would spoil everything if Elizabeth figured out The Plan now, after all they'd been through to keep it secret.

"The Wakefield party?" Mel asked, pulling out

a calendar. "No, you mean the Giardina party."

"No, I don't," Elizabeth said. "Remember? I'm Elizabeth Wakefield, and I'm hosting a surprise birthday party tonight for my twin sister, Jessica. You wrote it on your calendar when we booked the place."

"Today is the thirteenth," Enid said in her most helpful voice. "Look again, please."

Mel scrutinized his calendar again. "Nope. I got no record of a Wakefield party renting the place. I do have a private party for a movie star, Susie Giardina, who just won some award."

Elizabeth appeared to be having trouble catching her breath. Enid's heart went out to her, but she couldn't say anything or it would spoil the whole night. She bit her lip and stared at a spot on the wall behind Mel's balding head.

"There must be a mistake," Elizabeth choked out. "I gave you a deposit!"

"Look, here's the calendar," Mel told her. "See for yourself. 'Friday, June thirteenth: Giardina party.' No Wakefields, no birthdays, no twins. What you see is what you get." Enid felt her lips itching to smile. Mel deserved an Academy Award for this.

"But everyone at school already received the invitations!" Elizabeth cried, her eyes huge and terrified. "I invited over a hundred people because

146

you told me to! They'll all be coming here! Can't you cancel the other party?"

"Cancel? Why would I want to do that? Besides, this Susie Giardina has a contract and a lot of Hollywood connections. Sorry, kid, but you're out of luck."

Elizabeth took a deep, ragged breath, and Enid was afraid she would burst into tears. Enid closed her own eyes for a few seconds, pushing back her guilt over putting her best friend through this. Her face grew warm, and she hoped Elizabeth didn't notice that she was blushing.

"Come on, Elizabeth. Let's go," she said in a low voice.

As the girls turned to leave, Mel winked boldly at her, and Enid mentally rescinded his Academy Award. If Elizabeth had seen that wink, The Plan could be sunk. Elizabeth stared at Enid as they stepped outside into the late afternoon sun. "He winked at you! Why would he do that?"

Enid shrugged and tried to look nonchalant. "I guess you were right the last time. The guy was flirting. He obviously has a crush on me." Elizabeth stared at her oddly, and Enid thought she knew why. *Let's face it*, she told herself, *I'm no Jessica Wakefield.* She'd never been exactly deluged with guys showing interest. Then she realized

147

it wasn't Mel's apparent advances that had Elizabeth mystified but her own reaction to those advances. "Gross!" Enid added. "Why can't sleazy guys like that keep their winks to themselves?"

On the way to the car Elizabeth suddenly burst into tears. Enid felt queasy knowing that she was hurting her friend, even if it was all for a good reason.

"What are we going to do now?" Elizabeth cried. "All my planning just went down the toilet!"

Enid patted her arm sympathetically. "I'm so sorry, Liz."

"It's not your fault," Elizabeth said through her tears. "But now I'm totally clueless. How can I save Jessica's birthday? I wanted this to be perfect!"

Enid groped for words. "First, calm down. We'll think of something. We always do."

"What can we think of that will fix this?"

"I don't know yet. But I do know that a parking lot is not the best place for logical thinking. Let's go back to your house to regroup. I'm sure we'll come up with a new plan there."

Nodding automatically, Elizabeth allowed herself to be led to the car.

"How could this happen?" Jessica demanded desperately as she and Lila trudged back up the beach toward Lila's sports car.

Lila shook her head. "Maybe you should have done your homework about the rules for throwing parties on the beach."

"How was I supposed to know there were any rules to look up in the first place?" Jessica asked. "How could a person possibly know a thing like that?"

"It looks like your sister's party is toast," Lila lamented.

Jessica wrapped her arms around herself and tried to make sense of what had just happened. "Lila, did you know that Beach Patrol guy? The dark-haired one? He sure seemed to know you."

Lila raised her sunglasses and fixed Jessica with an amused stare. "Honestly, Jessica. Do you think I run in the same social circles as the guys who tell people not to throw trash on the beach?"

"But he kept giving you a weird look."

Lila put her hands on her hips. "Obviously the man wanted my body. That's why he was looking at me. Can you blame him?"

"It wasn't that kind of look." Jessica's brow creased in concentration. "It was more familiar, like he was trying to tell you something he knew you'd understand. What do you think it meant?"

"It meant that you've been conked on the head by that stupid tent one too many times," Lila said.

"Or that you're totally wigged out about this permit thing. Either way, you're hallucinating."

Jessica sighed. "Maybe, but I'm not giving up. The quartet is booked. We'll just have to move the party somewhere else. How about the grounds of Fowler Crest? We'll find a way to spread the word about it."

"Tell Amy Turbomouth Sutton," Lila suggested, checking her diamond-rimmed wristwatch. "The whole town will know in an hour flat."

A high-pitched beeping erupted from somewhere close by, startling Jessica. "What's that?"

"It's only my cellular phone," Lila informed her. "You must have jumped two feet in the air, girl. Chill out!"

"Who's calling at a time like this?"

"Yes, this is Lila," she said into the receiver. "Yes, it's so nice to speak with you again too. . . . Really? My father did? Well, I can understand that. . . . Oh, don't worry about us. We'll figure something out."

A profound sense of dread washed over Jessica, as deep as any ocean wave. "Who was that?"

Lila watched her face carefully. "That was your cellist."

"No!" Jessica screamed. "Lila, don't you dare tell me—"

"Your jazz combo canceled. My father asked them to play at a company function at the last minute."

"But you didn't even try to argue with her!"

Lila gave an exasperated sigh. "Duh! It's my father—as in the cellist's boss."

Jessica felt herself start to crumble. "My party is on the critical list, and you don't sound the least bit upset!"

"Hello! Your party was critical as soon as we got punted from the beach. What difference does the jazz quartet make at this point?"

"Are you sure it was your father's decision?" Jessica asked, outraged. "Are you sure you didn't have anything to do with it? Why are you sabotaging my birthday?"

Lila shook her head slowly. "I know you're under a lot of pressure right now, but you're waxing positively paranoid. You're hallucinating again."

"Is it so paranoid?" Jessica asked. "You've been AWOL for the last few days, changing your mind about helping—" Jessica stopped abruptly as the sand gave way beneath her feet. Suddenly the ocean roared. Its echoes thundered around them, and the whole world jerked violently, as if a rug had been snatched out from under them. Jessica grabbed Lila's arm and opened her mouth to scream.

"It's OK!" Lila yelled first. Already the earth was still and the rumbling sounds were fading. "It was only a little earthquake."

Jessica laughed weakly, but she was still breathing hard. "I've lived in California my whole life— you'd think I'd be used to them."

They watched the ocean curl back from the shore, farther back than Jessica had ever seen it, exposing a wide stripe of dirty, seaweed-strewn beach.

"This is way too creepy for words," Jessica said, pulling at Lila's arm. "Let's get out of here!" As they raced toward the parking lot she glanced back to see a mountain of water swelling offshore, a monstrous wave that suddenly let loose like something alive and wild and smashed against the beach. Then it rocked smoothly back into place, settling into the beach's usual rhythm of regular, moderate-size waves. Within minutes the ocean looked exactly the way it always did on a calm, clear day.

The girls were safe on the dry parking lot, but Lila's eyes were wide as she looked down over the beach. "That was one weird wave! I've never been on the beach during an earthquake before."

"I'm afraid to look," Jessica wailed. "Did it carry my rental tent out to sea?"

"Nope, it's still right where we left it. Your parents won't have to send your allowance to the party shop for the rest of your life."

"What about the party?"

"First things first," Lila said, pulling out her cell phone. "We obviously can't leave the tent on the beach without that stupid permit. But it won't fit in my Triumph."

"Who are you calling? I don't think the auto club jump-starts tents."

"I'm calling my father's driver," Lila informed her. "I'll have him pick up that canvas torture chamber in one of Dad's vans. In the meantime let's head over to your house to put on our party clothes."

"But what about the rest of my party?"

"Jessica, that party is so over," Lila said, rolling her eyes. "It's time to admit defeat and tell your sister the whole sordid little story."

"No! I'm not ready to give up! This is Elizabeth's surprise party we're talking about!"

"Whatever," Lila said in an impatient tone. "If you're pigheaded enough to still want to do the gala bash, then fine. Let's go back to your house to figure out how to salvage a birthday out of this. Either way, let's get out of here."

Elizabeth stared glumly out the window of the car, watching the neat suburban neighborhoods of Sweet Valley glide by. "Jessica is going to kill me!" she wailed to Enid. "The party at the Beach Disco is ruined, and I don't even have a present for her!"

"It's not your fault that—"

A loud bump interrupted Enid's sentence, followed by a burst of static from the radio. Enid clenched the steering wheel tightly with both hands, and the car wobbled as if it were on crutches.

"Enid!" Elizabeth cried. "What is it—a flat tire?"

Enid steered the hatchback onto the shoulder of the road, but the wobbling motion continued for several seconds after the car had stopped.

Elizabeth let out a relieved sigh when the motion ended. "It was just a minor earthquake. Nothing two California girls can't handle."

"I've been in earthquakes before, but never behind the wheel," Enid said.

"We should have expected it. After all, it is Friday the thirteenth."

"I feel the earth move under my feet. . . ." Enid sang the old song loudly in an obvious attempt to cheer Elizabeth.

Elizabeth couldn't manage more than a weak

smile. They sat in silence until the car turned onto Calico Drive. Even then Elizabeth was too lost in her thoughts to pay attention to the familiar houses of her own street.

"So tell me, is there anything else that can go wrong today?" she asked finally, hardly recognizing the bitter tone she heard coming out of her mouth. "How am I going to explain to Jessica that I was planning a terrific party for her, but that it went belly-up?"

Enid shrugged. "Don't beat yourself up over it. You tried. She'll appreciate that."

Elizabeth turned on her. "You don't even sound concerned! Don't you get it? I wanted to make this birthday special for her. But I can't think of a single way to fix this!"

"Parties and presents don't matter. The important thing is that you're together on your birthday," Enid said lamely.

"Tell that to Jessica!"

"Speaking of your other half," Enid said. "Isn't that Lila's car pulling into your driveway?"

Elizabeth blinked back her tears of frustration. "Yes, with Jessica right there beside her. I guess there's no other way to handle this. I've got to tell her the truth."

Enid pulled the hatchback into the driveway

next to the Triumph, but Lila and Jessica were still sitting in the car with the windows down, not moving. Elizabeth opened her door before Enid had turned off the car, and she heard a radio announcer's voice blaring out of Lila's stereo system. Enid flicked on her own radio.

"—the minor earthquake that hit southern California just a few minutes ago," the announcer was saying. "According to scientists with the U.S. Geological Survey, the temblor had a magnitude of 4.9 and was felt through much of southern California. Geologists say the epicenter was near the border between the towns of Bridgewater and Sweet Valley. There have been no reports of injuries or damage."

Jessica clambered out of the Triumph as soon as the radio announcer turned to a weather report. She wasn't ready to face Elizabeth. She just didn't know what to say. Besides, some small, optimistic part of her brain was still churning through possibilities, trying to come up with a way to go ahead with the surprise party for her sister.

"Jessica, I need to talk to you before—," Elizabeth was saying as she got out of Enid's car.

"Later," Jessica said abruptly. She slammed the car door behind her and began racing up the walkway, hoping to reach the house before Elizabeth caught up with her.

"Jess, please!" Elizabeth called behind her. "It's important."

Suddenly Lila was in front of her, clumsily blocking her way. "No, Li, I can't talk to her right now!" Jessica whispered.

Behind them she could hear Enid hurrying Elizabeth along until all four girls were standing on the front stoop together. In the distance she could hear the muffled staccato of Prince Albert's excited barking.

"Jessica, there's something I have to tell you," Elizabeth began.

Jessica's mind scrambled for a way to tell her sister the bad news—or better yet, to avoid telling her anything at all. "Not now, Elizabeth. Whatever it is, it can wait—"

Lila opened the front door and practically shoved Jessica inside while Enid shoved Elizabeth in just behind her. As they stumbled inside, the living room seemed to split apart in a kaleidoscope of noise, color, and light. Jessica had a swift impression of streamers, balloons, and a sea of friendly faces as an exuberant cheer enveloped the twins like a cloud of confetti.

"Surprise!"

Chapter 12

Elizabeth's head was spinning as her friends and family hugged and congratulated her. "How in the—," she began weakly, but her voice trailed off when she felt someone tugging on her arm. Jessica was at her side, eyes wide.

"Lizzie, did you—"

"I wanted to," Elizabeth admitted, raising her voice to be heard above the din. "I planned a party at the Beach Disco. But everything went wrong and—"

Jessica shook her head in disbelief. "But I—"

Enid and Lila steered them to the couch, and Elizabeth was grateful to sit down beside her sister. Her parents materialized out of the crowd, and her mother handed her a glass of punch. Then Elizabeth nearly jumped out of her skin when a saxophone began playing "My Favorite Things" somewhere nearby.

"A jazz quartet!" she cried, seeing through a break in the crowd that four musicians were set up in the corner. "I don't understand! How did all this happen?"

"We confess!" Enid cried gleefully, wrapping an arm around Lila, of all people. Elizabeth stared.

"Jessica planned a party for Elizabeth," Lila explained. "But Elizabeth planned one for Jessica at the same time—"

"Your friends didn't want to spoil either surprise—," Mrs. Wakefield added.

"So they sabotaged both parties and planned a joint one of their own!" Steven concluded, leaning over to kiss both twins on the cheek.

"Happy birthday!" Enid and Lila shouted together. Then Enid hugged Elizabeth, and Lila hugged Jessica.

"Combining the parties was Lila's idea," Enid told them. "Jessica had booked the jazz combo, so we put them here in the living room to provide some ambience indoors."

"And the Droids should be setting up out near the pool," Lila added.

"The Droids!" Jessica shrieked. "You hired the Droids? Lila, you're a genius."

"Actually the Droids were Enid's idea," Lila admitted.

"This is totally awesome!" Jessica breathed. Suddenly her eyes filled with horror.

Elizabeth grabbed her arm. "Jess, what is it?"

"My outfit!" Jessica screamed. For the first time Elizabeth noticed she was wearing a huge T-shirt and biker shorts, both covered with sand. "Lila, you knew I'd be dressed for setting up that stupid tent on the beach!" Jessica complained. "How could you let me come to a party like this?"

"Chill out, Jess. I'm totally grody too. Remember, we're at your house! Let's go upstairs and change. Then it's time to party!"

As Jessica and Lila ran upstairs Elizabeth glanced down briefly at her own black jeans and fuchsia blouse.

"You look beautiful, sweetheart," her father assured her.

"At this point I don't care in the least," Elizabeth said with a grin. "This party is the biggest and best surprise of my life, and I'm going to have a blast, no matter what I'm wearing. Thank you, everyone!"

"Don't worry about us old folks hanging around to cramp your style," Mrs. Wakefield said with a laugh. "Your father and I will be out of here within the hour. We're going out to dinner and a movie."

"You two don't have to leave!" Elizabeth said. "We'd love to have you here for the party!"

"Thank you, but I'm not sure your sister would second that invitation," Mr. Wakefield said, his brown eyes twinkling.

"Don't anybody worry," Steven told everyone. "When Mom and Dad leave, Billie and I will be here as your official birthday chaperons."

"That is so reassuring," Winston said in a squeaky falsetto. "Personally, I feel much safer just knowing that Steven and Billie are on the job!" He had just popped over with Maria Slater and Olivia to congratulate Elizabeth. They pulled her and Enid into the kitchen, where the music wasn't quite as loud.

"Happy seventeenth, Liz!" Olivia said, giving her a hug. Olivia was smiling, but Elizabeth noticed there were circles under her friend's eyes. She resolved to corner Olivia later and make sure she was all right.

Winston gazed at Elizabeth with a mock-serious expression. "Do you realize, Elizabeth, that you've already lived twenty-one and one-quarter percent of your entire life expectancy?"

"No way, Winston," Maria Slater chimed in. "Twins live twice as long!"

"This is fantastic!" Elizabeth exclaimed. "It looks like every person in our class is here!"

"I don't think anyone ended up taking RSVPs in the end," Enid said. "But practically everyone who was invited to either party—or both parties— seems to be here!"

"Speaking of which, has anyone, uh, seen Maria?" Winston asked.

"I saw her out by the pool a few minutes ago, helping Dana and the Droids with their sound equipment," Olivia said.

Bruce Patman breezed into the kitchen and patted Elizabeth on the shoulder. "So the Wakefield twins are seventeen years old. Almost all grown up, huh?" he remarked sarcastically.

"That's Bruce's way of saying happy birthday," Maria explained.

Bruce poured two sodas and sauntered off toward the living room, and Elizabeth turned to Enid and asked in a low voice, "Is Todd here?"

Enid bit her lip. "I don't know if he's coming, Liz," she admitted. "The truth is, I kind of doubt it. He's still pretty upset."

Elizabeth squeezed her arm. "Don't worry about it. I refuse to be bummed out tonight. This is a time for celebration, not for looking back on things I screwed up in the past! Besides, everyone else I care about is here!"

"Even Prince Albert," Enid said with a laugh. "At least, I hear *somebody* barking like crazy in the basement!"

"Poor doggie. Maybe we'll let him come out to join the party later," Elizabeth said. "It's not like it could really be any noisier in here!"

From the living room bounced the cheerful opening of "In the Mood." Maria grabbed Elizabeth's arm, and together they danced around the room.

The house was entirely too quiet. Todd reached for the remote control and pointed it in the direction of the large-screen television set in his family's multimedia room. He flipped through a half dozen stations before he let it rest on the Dodgers game, then punched up the volume until sound filled the room. Unfortunately the roar of the crowd did nothing to raise his spirits.

Todd caught sight of one of the hot pink flyers that Lila, Enid, and the others had made up, informing the twins' friends of The Plan for one big party to take the place of the two that Jessica and Elizabeth had been planning. He checked his watch. The party had started by now. Elizabeth was at her house, surrounded by her family and her friends. He wondered briefly if Devon Whitelaw was there but banished the thought from his mind. As Todd grabbed the remote and clicked up the volume of the baseball game another notch, he slumped back into the soft cushions of the couch.

Todd sighed. His parents were driving to Los Angeles to see a play that night, so he was alone in the house. And every one of his friends was on Calico Drive, partying it up with the Wakefield twins. He imagined teenagers overflowing the split-level house and yard, music blaring, and everyone gabbing and laughing about the end of the school year. He always hated to miss a good blowout. Even the Dodgers were losing.

Todd leaned forward and grabbed the other sheet of paper from the coffee table. It was a letter he'd received that day, on crisp, white letterhead. The letter should have made him happy. He *was* happy about it, he told himself. It was a great opportunity, and it meant he didn't have to spend his summer moping around town, infecting all his friends with his rotten mood.

"My friends," he said aloud. He knew they really cared about what he was going through.

Enid had cornered him during study hall that day, still trying to change his mind about attend-

ing the birthday party. Winston had called and offered to lend him a pair of dark sunglasses—in
case he wanted to come incognito. Ken and Aaron
had stopped by on their way to the Wakefields',
urging him to join them. They'd even offered to
skip the celebration and watch baseball with him
if he didn't want to be alone.

The letter he was holding in his hands meant
he wouldn't see any of them for two months, starting right after exams and graduation. Tonight was
everyone's chance to say good-bye for the summer,
and Todd was spending the evening alone. In his
heart he knew he was making the right decision
about the summer, but suddenly he felt about as
bummed out as he'd ever been.

"What am I doing?" he asked over the baseball
announcer's voice. "I shouldn't be here. I should
be with my friends!"

Jessica strolled down the stairs ahead of Lila
into air charged with the scents of perfume, salsa,
and minipizzas. She was dressed for making a grand
entrance, in the formfitting turquoise minidress
she'd been coveting for weeks at the mall. The
dress had been waiting in her bedroom, a gift from
Lila and Amy, and it looked even more gorgeous
now than it had in Lisette's display window. Jessica

tossed her head to make her tousled hair fall around her face in sexy waves. But with all the people and happy confusion downstairs, she wasn't sure if anyone would even notice her.

She heard a whistle and turned toward it. Bruce raised his soda can in a silent toast to Jessica and winked. His face bore its usual smug expression, but she figured she'd just received the biggest compliment somebody as arrogant as Bruce could manage, so she smiled back at him.

"Looking good, Wakefield!" Ken called out.

Winston fell to his knees at the bottom of the steps. "Marry me!" he pleaded.

She kicked him lightly with her high-heeled shoe as if to move him aside. But her excitement rose with every compliment. She turned to Lila and gave her a high five. "This is going to be one serious party!"

As Jessica reached the hallway outside the living room she realized she couldn't hear the Droids from the backyard, so she figured they hadn't yet begun to play. As the jazz quartet finished a fast dance number Mr. Wakefield motioned for quiet, with no discernible results. Mrs. Wakefield tapped on a glass with a fork, and the chaos dulled to a low hum.

"The twins' mother and I have an announcement to make," Mr. Wakefield called out as

Elizabeth emerged from the kitchen with a large group of guests. More people squeezed into the room as he spoke. "We senior citizens plan to clear out of here before the punk band starts to play," he said. "But before we do, we have a very special presentation."

"Birthday presents!" Jessica squealed.

"Birthday present, singular," her mother corrected. "But I think you'll be happy to share this one." She whispered something to Steven, who immediately disappeared out the front door.

Elizabeth stood next to Jessica. They grasped hands as their parents waited for another group of guests to push its way into the room. Practically everyone they knew were there. Amy reached out and patted her on the shoulder. Jade and Sara were grinning from ear to ear. Jessica caught a glimpse of Devon's dark brown hair, but he faded back into the crowd, and she didn't think Elizabeth had seen him.

"Jess, you look amazing!" Elizabeth whispered in her ear.

Jessica squeezed her hand. "So do you," she replied with complete sincerity. Today the glow of happiness in her sister's eyes made her look prettier than any amount of makeup could. Jessica saw her fingering her gold lavaliere necklace and then noticed with a chuckle that she herself was holding on to the identical one around her own neck. The twins' parents had given them the necklaces exactly one year ago on their sixteenth birthday.

Mrs. Wakefield held up a small box wrapped in gold paper. Jessica was confused. *Only jewelry comes in boxes that little,* she thought. *But there's no way they'd buy us one piece of jewelry to share!* "The package may look small on the outside," their mother said, "but I think you'll find it's much bigger on the inside!"

Jessica and Elizabeth stared at each other, perplexed. When Mrs. Wakefield handed them the box, they opened it together.

"Car keys!" Jessica shrieked, jingling them in the air.

Elizabeth's mouth dropped open. "Mom, Dad? Does this mean what I think it means?"

Their parents threw open the front door. Steven stood near the garage door, where he'd just backed a sparkling white Jeep out into the driveway, ahead of Lila and Enid's cars.

"A new Jeep! We have a new Jeep!" Jessica cried, running to the door and jumping up and down. Her heart was pounding so hard, she thought she might hyperventilate. As everyone began talking at once she whirled to see Elizabeth throw her arms around their mother. Then Jessica tackled Mr. Wakefield in a flying leap of a hug.

The quartet began playing a jazzed-up version of "Happy Birthday to You," and everyone started to sing. Even Prince Albert joined in, his muffled howls echoing up from the basement. Joyful tears sprang to Jessica's eyes and were mirrored on her sister's face. "This," she whispered to Elizabeth, "is the happiest birthday ever!"

As Winston sang along with the others his eyes scanned the colorful crowd, searching for a petite figure with a pretty face and a head of long, dark hair. It was great to see the twins so stoked, but he couldn't completely share in the festive mood—not with his own life in such a mess. Maria Santelli had been avoiding him ever since he'd arrived at the Wakefield house. He'd seen only glimpses of her, disappearing around a corner or into a crowd. He was sure she was intentionally avoiding him, and he knew he couldn't go on this way. He had to talk to her.

He spotted her near the entrance to the kitchen and maneuvered through the crowded hallway until he could slip behind her. The instant the song ended and everyone else began talking and laughing again, he took Maria's arm and spun her to face him.

"Winston!" she cried.

"Please, Maria, I've got to talk to you. Just give me two minutes." Before she could protest, he pulled her into the kitchen and around the corner to the basement stairs. He slipped through the stairwell door, dragging Maria along, and shut it behind them before Prince Albert could escape. At the top of the steps the golden retriever jumped on him, nearly knocking Winston over.

Maria grabbed his arm to keep him from falling down the stairs. Despite the near miss, the familiar warmth of her fingers through his cotton shirt sent ripples of joy through his body. For a moment Maria stared at her hand on his arm. In the light of the bulb overhead he saw a blush spreading over her face. She jerked her hand away as if she'd been burned.

Prince Albert jumped on him again. "Get down, dog breath!" Winston ordered. "Can't you see we're standing at the top of a staircase? Your jumping could be hazardous to our health!"

"Winston, what is this about?" Maria asked in a faint voice as Winston held on to the dog's collar to keep him from jumping again.

"Maria, I'm sorry!" Winston exclaimed. "That's what it's about."

"Winston—"

"Please, just hear me out. After I've said what I need to say, if you want me to go away and leave you alone, I will. You won't ever have to talk to me again!"

"You don't have to—"

"I'm sorry I couldn't keep my big mouth shut!" he interrupted. "I'm sorry I embarrassed you, and more than anything, I'm sorry I made you think you couldn't trust me. I know I was a jerk and I don't deserve someone like you. But I love you, and I can't stand the thought of you being mad at me."

"What is it you want, Winston?" Maria said with a sigh. "If you want me to say I forgive you, OK. I guess I do. But I still—"

"I want you to take me back!" he cried, louder than he'd intended. Prince Albert barked sharply. "Please, please, please take me back!" Winston begged. "If you want me to keep my mouth shut, just tell me. I swear I'll never say another word! As long as we can be together, that's all that matters."

Maria leaned against the door, staring down the steps at nothing. "I love you too, but I—"

"You love me!" Winston cried. "That's fantastic. We can work with that. Please, Maria. Think about all the fun times we've had. Think about the pizza-eating contests at Guido's, and the late night student council projects, and the jokes you helped me play on Patman. . . ."

Maria smiled, and Winston's heart leaped. *She actually smiled!*

"You do always make me laugh like nobody else can," she admitted. "I'd probably hate it if you swore to keep your mouth shut."

"Does that mean you'll take me back?" He put his hand on her shoulder, and this time she didn't pull away from the contact. "I think you'd better answer fast, Maria, before I have a heart attack. My pulse is pounding so loud, I bet you can hear it all over the house!"

Maria laughed. "That's not your pulse, silly. The Droids just started playing out back." Prince Albert howled.

"Maybe, but my heart's drumming to beat the band," Winston said, trying to decide if Maria's smile meant what he thought it meant. "So, are we are a couple again? Or do I have to throw myself down these stairs, where my mangled body will meet its bloody death far below, at the bottom of this dark abyss?"

"Winston, the bottom's about eight feet away."

"I was speaking metaphorically."

Maria shook her head, but her eyes were twinkling. "Well, it may be a pretty lame abyss, but I wouldn't want you to sprain an ankle or anything on the way down. So if those are my only options, I guess we're a couple again."

"Wahoo!" Winston shrieked, dropping Prince Albert's collar to throw both arms around Maria. The dog immediately jumped against his back, nearly toppling them both.

"I do have one condition," Maria said after they'd regained their balance.

Winston bowed with a flourish. "Anything, my queen."

"Promise me you'll watch your mouth from now on."

Winston pantomimed locking his lips and throwing away the key. Then Maria's lips touched his. And for the first time in his life, Winston couldn't think of a single thing he wanted to say.

Chapter 13

Dana Larson was belting out an original tune called "Double Trouble," written in honor of the Wakefield girls. To Bruce her sultry voice actually seemed to raise the temperature of the warm June night. Occasional stabs of heat lightning flashed against distant clouds, but the weather forecast said rain would hold off until at least tomorrow. A row of tiny garden lanterns lined one edge of the patio around the pool, their votive candles flickering yellow behind patterns of cutwork tin.

Bruce was psyched about the evening. Ever since the twins' parents had left a half hour earlier, the Droids had been blasting industrial punk. The din was properly earsplitting in the backyard, but with the sliding glass doors closed the quartet could play jazz in the living room without being drowned out. Bruce had been alternating his time between the more elegant ambience inside and the electrified atmosphere of the back patio. But as the party wore on and the aroma of chicken on the barbecue grill wafted through the house, more and more of the partyers congregated out back.

Watching the growing crowd, Bruce came to a decision. He'd spent enough time out of the spotlight. Besides, he had news to tell. All his friends still thought he was going to Harvard. It was time to set the record straight. So when Dana finished her song, he asked if he could borrow her microphone. Then he jumped onto the makeshift stage.

"Hey, guys! Listen up," Bruce ordered. Faces turned toward him. "I've got an announcement to make—some late-breaking news to make you wish, once again, that you were me."

"As if!" Lila whispered to Jessica, loud enough for Bruce to hear.

I rest my case, Bruce thought. But he had more important issues than Lila Fowler's sour grapes. "Everyone's heard I'm going to Harvard next year, but I wanted you all to be the first to know that I've changed my mind."

"I hope you've changed it into something useful!" Winston called back to him. Winston and

Maria Santelli stood so close together that they looked like Siamese twins—albeit a strange pair, with gangly, goofy-looking Winston towering over the small, pretty cheerleader. Bruce was surprised to see them so chummy; he'd thought they'd broken up. But Winston's pathetic little love life wasn't worth speculating about. His own life was much more interesting.

"Not surprisingly, Sweet Valley University has accepted me into the incoming freshman class," Bruce continued. *Not at all surprising—considering the fact that Dad just donated a new wing for the library,* he thought. But he wasn't about to tell his friends that part. "And I've decided to accept SVU's offer."

"S-V-U!" Steven and Billie yelled together, as if they were at a football game. Some of the others called out encouragement, congratulations, or disparaging jokes.

"Sure, there's mourning in Cambridge, Massachusetts, tonight," Bruce continued with mock sadness. "But as far as I'm concerned . . ." He paused for effect, then held the microphone close to his mouth for maximum volume. "New England is just too darn *cold!*"

This time everyone cheered. As Bruce stepped down, the Droids started in on their punk version of "California Dreaming."

*　　*　　*

The back door opened, and Olivia startled as a loud, percussive version of "California Dreaming" streamed into the crowded kitchen like a search-light. Billie walked in from the patio, carrying an empty ice bucket. The rock music snapped off when Billie pulled the door shut behind her and was replaced again by the lighter strains of bebop that sparkled from the living room. Olivia held a large flat package against her body, grasping it with tense fingers as she scanned the kitchen, looking for a tall, lean boy with blond hair and deep-set eyes.

She'd just retrieved the painting from her car, and she was nervous. "I'm making the right deci-sion," she whispered to herself.

"Did you say something?" asked Maria Santelli, who was standing at the counter, refilling a salsa bowl and raving with Annie Whitman about how well the party was going.

"I was just talking to myself," Olivia said with a self-deprecating grin. "You know how crazy we artists can be."

Winston emerged from the basement door, hold-ing an agitated Prince Albert on a short leash. "This dog has lived with Jessica too long! He's gone com-pletely and utterly bananas!" The golden retriever twisted and jumped so that Winston had to grab on with both hands just to keep hold of him.

"I think he's in the mood for punk music instead of jazz," Billie decided. "See? He's trying to dance!"

Prince Albert howled, and conversation in the kitchen faded momentarily.

"Well, I'm glad you brought him up from the basement," Maria said. "It was breaking my heart, hearing him scrabbling at the door. Maybe he just wants to join the party."

"Liz says there's some doggie treats in the pantry," Winston said. "I thought I'd see if bribery will calm him down for a while." He dragged the golden retriever into the pantry and pulled the door shut behind him.

Billie opened the freezer and scanned its contents. "Anyone know if there's more ice anywhere?" she asked. "We've just about gone through the bags in the coolers out back."

"Oops," Maria said. "That's all the ice we brought. Sounds like we miscalculated big time."

"Oops is right," Winston agreed, emerging from the pantry, Prince Albert in tow, in time to hear Maria's reply. The dog was crunching a biscuit but still seemed agitated. "Never fear," Winston assured them, struggling to hold on to the dog. "The iceman cometh. I'll maketh a grocery store run, and your coolers will runneth over."

Maria smiled and kissed him on the cheek. "Thanks, Win. And hurryeth back. We need the ice—besides, the party won't be the sameth without you."

Winston grinned his widest, goofiest grin, and Olivia sighed. It was nice to see Maria and Winston back together again. She hoped desperately that she and Ken would be standing together, smiling at each other just like that, before the night was over.

"I'll just find a place to stash the pooch, and then I'm off," Winston said. "But I'll be back in a flash." He slapped his forehead with his palm. "Hello! Make that a long flash. I just remembered that this iceman had to parketh his chariot six blocks away."

"Don't worry about it," Billie said, pulling a set of car keys from her pocket and dangling them in the air. "I'll make the ice run. Steven's Volkswagen is parked right out front, and I've got his keys."

"Are you sure that's a good plan?" Winston asked. "Steven's Bug looks like it's reaching new heights of falling-apartness."

"Right," Maria said with a laugh. "Like your VW is in any better shape, Winston. It's just as ancient as Steven's."

"True, but mine is orange. Everyone knows that an orange VW Bug lasts longer than a yellow one."

"Steven's yellow Bug got us here from the university this morning," Billie said. "I'm sure it can handle the two miles to the grocery store."

"Billie, you know Ken Matthews, don't you?" Olivia asked. "I can't find him anywhere. He may have gone outside to his car. If you run into him out front, would you tell him I'm looking for him?"

"Sure thing," Billie said.

Annie turned to Billie. "Do you want us to tell Steven where you're going?"

"I'll tell him myself when I grab the coolers from the patio to bring along," Billie replied. With a wave and a smile she left the kitchen to a burst of punk music. Prince Albert barked and strained against Winston's grasp on his collar. The door closed, and the Droids' latest song winked out like a light.

"No way, fellow!" Winston called above the dog's howls. "You are not joining the party outside. It's back in the pantry for you. How about another one of those hard-as-rock biscuits you like so much?"

"It shut him up for a whole three minutes last time," Maria said with a laugh.

Winston shrugged. "There's at least ten biscuits

left in the package. At three minutes of silence apiece, I can keep this dog occupied for a good half hour. . . . Maybe I should have asked Billie to pick up another box."

After Winston and the dog disappeared into the pantry, Annie pointed to the square, flat package Olivia was clenching. "That must be a special birthday present for the twins."

Olivia shrugged. "Not exactly," she said, looking away. "The truth is, it's kind of an end-of-the-year thing for Ken."

"I thought you two were . . ." Annie bit her lip.

"We are. I was hoping I could change his mind," Olivia said. "If I can find him, that is."

"I'm sure he went through here a few minutes ago," Maria said.

Annie pointed toward the front of the house. "He headed thataway. I bet he's in the living room."

Olivia hugged the package close to her body. "I hope he didn't leave the party early," she said. "I was so nervous about talking to him, and now it might be too late."

"Ken never left a party early in his life," Maria assured her. "You'll find him."

Olivia nodded her thanks and headed for the hallway. At the foot of the staircase Amy Sutton

181

leaned against the wall, flirting mildly with Danny Porter.

"Has either of you seen Ken?" Olivia asked.

Amy rolled her wide gray eyes. Olivia knew the blond cheerleader thought Ken was way out of Olivia's league. Amy cocked her head toward the living room, her long straight hair shimmering like a shampoo commercial. "He was heading in that direction last time I saw him."

Olivia edged past them and stopped at the entrance to the living room. Cheryl Thomas, Annie's stepsister and a talented pianist, sat cross-legged on the floor directly in front of the musicians. Her eyes were riveted on the keyboard player, and her fingers played an invisible piano in her lap. Two seniors Olivia barely knew were slow dancing despite the peppy song. In the corner near the fireplace Jade, Aaron, Penny, David Prentiss, and Maria Slater were holding an animated discussion. But Ken was nowhere to be found.

Olivia walked to the window. Pulling aside the sheer curtain, she peered down the street to the next block, where she'd seen Ken's Toyota earlier. She couldn't see the white car now. *He must have gone home,* she decided, blinking back tears.

She stared out at the sky over Calico Drive. *Star light, star bright,* she thought mechanically, and then shook her head. There wasn't a single star to wish on. Clouds had been gathering all afternoon, and now the sky was an unbroken expanse of sooty black. If she could have just one wish, Olivia knew exactly what it would be. But Ken was gone. No wishes would come true tonight. Her hands suddenly felt cold and bloodless around the wrapped painting.

Suddenly something moved outside close to the house. Not caring what the other party guests thought, she knelt on the couch, her face almost against the window, for a sidelong view of the front steps. Someone was there. A tall boy was sitting on the doorstep, the moonlight playing on his broad-shouldered back and glimmering off a head of blond hair. From the back, with his head in his hands, he looked dejected and vulnerable. She took a deep breath. Then she jumped up from the couch, her hands still clenched around Ken's present.

Olivia slipped out the door and shut it soundlessly behind her. Outside, the warm night was a confusion of sound. A muffled saxophone solo from inside the house wafted around her like smoke, but it vied with the driving beat of one of Dana's original punk numbers from the backyard. A cat wailed in the dark. And a black shadow skidded across the dark gray of the Wakefields' front lawn. A fixture by the door bathed the front steps in a garish light that made Olivia think of a Van Gogh painting of a café at night, filled with hopeless people.

"Ken?" she said in a low voice, gazing at the back of his head as he sat motionless on the front step. "Can we talk?"

His back stiffened. "What more is there to say?"

She sat beside him on the step, not quite touching him. Ken stared at her for a moment, but his eyes moved down to the package resting against her knees, and he turned away. "I don't believe this!" he fumed. "How could you bring that here?"

"It's not what you think!"

"I guess humiliating me at the art show isn't enough, so you're giving our friends a sneak preview tonight!"

She pushed the package toward him. "Here, I want you to open it."

"Here? Are you nuts?"

"Please, Ken. You've got to trust me on this."

He shoved the package back. "The way I trusted you when you said you wanted to paint my portrait?"

Olivia felt a tear slide down her face, and she scrubbed it away with her sleeve. "I was so caught up in defending my freedom of expression that I didn't stop to think about how it was affecting you. You were asking me to choose between my art and my love for you, and that made me so angry—"

"What about the choice you were asking of me?" Ken demanded.

"I know," Olivia admitted. "I've thought about this a lot, Ken. I see now that it was just as unfair to ask you to choose between your pride and your feelings for me."

"If both our choices are impossible to make, then where does that leave us? If you can't pass the ball and you can't run with it, the only thing you can do is throw it away!"

Olivia stared at the starless sky. "Is that what you want, Ken? To throw away everything we've got?"

"What else is there to do? Whether you shred that painting or put it in the art show, one of us feels screwed. Either you can't . . . I don't know . . . face yourself as an artist or whatever. Or I can't face anyone in town! How can we stay together after that?"

"I don't know much about football," Olivia began haltingly. "But in art, maybe there's another option besides throwing the ball away."

Ken scowled. "I don't get it."

"If you don't like your options in art, you can throw a second ball onto the field," Olivia said. She pushed the wrapped painting at him again, and this time she took his hand in hers and placed it on the package. "Open it, Ken. Please."

Ken stared at her for what seemed like a full minute. Then he gingerly pulled the wrapping off one end of the painting—just far enough to look inside. He raised his eyebrows incredulously and then stared at Olivia. "Is this what I think it is?"

Olivia nodded, and Ken tore off the rest of the wrapping. The painting inside was a new one, similar to the original but in a close-up view, showing only Ken's head and shoulders against the same gardenlike background. "You redid it!"

"If you like it, I want you to keep this one as a gift," Olivia told him. "But first—if you agree—this is the portrait I'll give Ms. Markey to put in the exhibit next week."

"And the other painting?"

Olivia looked at her hands in her lap. "I planned to destroy the original, like you wanted. But when it came down to it, Ken, I just couldn't do it." She gazed into his eyes and felt her own filling with tears. "You may think there's too much of *you* in that painting," she said, and smiled weakly. "But the truth is, there's an awful lot of *me* in it."

"So what are you suggesting instead?" Ken asked. "I can't risk anybody I know ever getting hold of that picture."

"Let me hang on to it, in the bottom of a drawer somewhere," Olivia replied. "I swear on a stack of Rembrandts that I will never show it to anyone as long as I live—or as long as you don't want me to. You can trust me on that."

"But you said I have no right to decide what should happen to that painting."

"You don't have the right to force to destroy it against my will," Olivia said care. But you wouldn't be forcing me. Ken, I love you, and I want you to feel OK with this decision. If you insist, I'll somehow find the guts to take a knife to that thing."

"You would do that for me?"

Olivia sniffed. "If I have to. But I'm asking you not to insist."

Ken stared at the night sky, clenching and unclenching his hands in his lap. He picked up the new portrait again, the one that showed only his head and shoulders. Finally he looked at Olivia. "Here's the deal."

Olivia stared at him, tears sparkling in her eyes.

"This painting, the G-rated one, is terrific. Livy, I really love it."

"You do?" she breathed.

"Absolutely. I *want* you to put it in the art show next week. It's amazing, thinking that my face is on a work of art! After that I do want to keep it. But every time I look at it, it'll be your face I see."

Olivia beamed through her tears. "And the original portrait?" she asked after a moment, her voice steady.

Ken took a deep breath. "I can't ask you to destroy it. It's yours to keep or slash to pieces."

"You really mean that?"

"I won't even ask about that portrait again—as long as I have your word that nobody will ever see it without my permission."

"I promise," Olivia said. "Thanks for trusting me."

She threw her arms around him, but Ken gently held her away. "I need one more promise from you," he told her.

Olivia bit her lip. "What?"

"Promise me that we will never have another fight about anything, ever again. And that you'll always love me, no matter what."

Olivia ruffled a hand through his thick blond hair. "Only if it's a mutual pact."

"I wouldn't have it any other way," he said, pulling her close. Their lips met, and Olivia felt the pain and longing of the past ten days sliding away like an outgoing tide. Ken was kissing her ardently, passionately—as if it were the last time. And Olivia responded, thrilling to the salty-sweet taste of his mouth, the caress of his hands on her back, the strength of his body against hers. She had never felt so warm and alive.

Then the sound of footsteps ripped through their euphoria, and Olivia and Ken jumped apart, blushing. A dark figure was trudging up the front walk.

"Sorry, guys," said Todd's voice a moment before he emerged into the circle of yellow light.

"Wilkins, it's you!" Ken said, catching his breath. "Don't worry about it, dude. Glad you decided to come."

"It's all right, Todd," Olivia said. "I didn't see your car pull up."

Todd raised his eyebrows. "I could have driven up in an armored tank, and I doubt either of you would have noticed a thing."

"We were, uh . . . distracted," Ken replied.

"Actually," Todd said, "I had to park the Beemer four blocks down!"

"It does seem as if half the cars in Sweet Valley are along Calico Drive right now," Olivia admitted.

"I thought this party was a surprise," Todd said.

"Weren't all the cars a dead giveaway?"

Olivia shrugged. "Nobody was allowed to park within two blocks until after the twins arrived. I guess some people moved their cars later."

"The place looks like the inside of a sardine can," Ken said, "but with music."

"It's a blast," Olivia said. "But things haven't been the same, Todd, without you here as one of the gang."

"You two didn't look like you were missing me much when I walked up!" Todd said with a lop-sided smile.

Ken shrugged, grinning back. "Maybe not at that precise moment."

"I'm glad you worked things out." Todd's eyes kept darting around the front yard. He wrung his hands together in front of him, then shoved them in his pockets, and Olivia realized he was as afraid of facing his former girlfriend as Elizabeth was of facing him. Todd nodded toward the house— which still emanated overlapping jazz and punk, with an occasional dog bark for percussion. "It sounds like a wild bash!"

"It's had its ups and downs," Olivia admitted. "Todd, I know how hard it was for you to come tonight, but it'll mean a lot to Elizabeth that you did."

Todd stared at the pavement. "I can't go on avoiding Liz," he told them. "We've put this off for too long. Do you have any idea where I can find her?"

Olivia nodded. "The last time I looked, she was out back, taking a turn at the barbecue grill."

"Go on, dude!" Ken ordered. "Talk to her."

"Thanks, man," Todd said, reaching for the doorknob. "I'll just go inside and let you two . . . go back to, uh, whatever you were doing."

Todd disappeared inside in a burst of bebop, and Olivia snuggled back into Ken's arms.

"So, Freeverse," Ken said in a soft, warm voice as he tousled her hair. Olivia smiled at the mention of her chat-room screen name, and Ken continued speaking. "Does this mean our relationship is back on-line?"

"Yes, Quarter, that's exactly what it means!" Olivia replied. "And all of a sudden life is virtually perfect!"

Ken groaned at her joke, a pained look on his face. "Despite that totally fatal pun . . . I really do love you, Olivia."

She locked her arms around his waist and wished she could hold on forever. "I love you too."

Chapter 14

Onstage, Max Dellon's electric guitar screamed through a discordant chord progression while Dana bellowed the lyrics to one of her original punk songs, "Pierced and Proud." Directly in front of an amplifier Jessica danced energetically to the driving beat, liking the feel of her hair bouncing against her shoulders as the rhythms vibrated through her body.

"Radical tune!" Andy Jenkins, her dance partner, yelled into her ear.

Jessica, breathing hard from her exertions, gave him a thumbs-up sign. Suddenly a strong hand grasped her shoulder. Jessica grinned. Andy was a great guy and a total babe. But being cut in on always gave her a thrill. She shrugged apologetically at Andy and turned to see who her new dance partner was.

"Steven!" she cried. She wouldn't have minded dancing one song with her brother. After all, it was her birthday. But he knew better than to cut in when she was with somebody cute. She gestured to Andy that she'd only be a moment. "Can't you see I'm busy?" she yelled into her brother's ear.

"No problem," Steven yelled back. "I just need to borrow the keys to the Jeep."

Jessica hooted with laughter. "Not in this lifetime."

"It's an emergency, Jess," Steven insisted, pulling her away from the amplifier. "Billie just called from the store. She was on an ice run, and the Volkswagen died. I have to go pick her up."

"Pick her up in something else," Jessica said. "There's no way you're driving my new Jeep before I do!"

"Get a life. What difference does it make if I drive it first?"

"It's *my* Jeep, and I'm going to be the first person behind the wheel!" Jessica insisted. "It's only fair."

"The Jeep's already been driven by someone else," Steven pointed out. "How do you think Mom and Dad got it here in the first place? By airlift?"

"That doesn't count! It wasn't mine yet."

"Yours?" Steven asked. "Aren't you forgetting Clone Number One, the Jeep's co-owner?"

Jessica put her hands on her hips. She hated it when Steven called her and her sister The Clones. "Elizabeth doesn't care about stuff like being first," she said impatiently, surprised that someone who was smart enough to take prelaw classes couldn't understand such a simple concept. "She knows it's more important to me. Why else would she have let me hang on to the keys?"

"Get over it, Jessica," Steven said. "Billie is stranded."

Jessica sighed heavily, rolling her eyes. "All right, don't wig on me. It'll mean leaving my own birthday party, so you owe me."

Steven reached for the keys, but Jessica pulled her hand away. "We'll go pick up Billie together," she said firmly. "*I'm* driving."

"Fine," Steven said, taking her arm and yanking her toward the side of the house. "Let's go."

Jessica stopped and crossed her arms. "Not so fast! Have you seen Lila anywhere? I can't get the Jeep out until she moves her car."

"I'll tell Liz where we're going," Steven said, gesturing to the far side of the pool. Jessica followed his gaze. Through a break in the crowd she saw her sister laying chicken legs on the barbecue grill. "You go find Lila," he told her.

Jessica narrowed her eyes at him. Since when was he giving orders? "Yes, *sir!*" she yelled sarcastically, saluting. "I'll meet you in the driveway in five minutes, *sir!*"

Devon sat in the grass at the edge of the lighted area of the Wakefields' backyard. He turned a gift-wrapped package over and over in his hands, wondering if the present he'd chosen for Elizabeth was a mistake.

He watched her on the patio near the pool, leaning over the barbecue grill. She'd rolled up the sleeves of her blouse, and her arms were slender and deeply tanned. The glow from the coals cast a rosy light over her face and hair. Penny stopped by the barbecue grill, and Elizabeth's features lit with laughter at something her friend told her.

When Devon saw Elizabeth this way, happy and beautiful, he had a hokey, sentimental urge to shower her with gifts, the kinds of gifts that would prove his love. As he gazed at her he imagined himself offering her a different gift from the one in the package he now held. . . .

Their fingers would touch with an almost electric charge as he handed her a box wrapped in shiny silver paper with a ridiculously elaborate bow. Her blue-green eyes would sparkle with excitement as she opened the box and pulled out . . . something. He didn't know what—a ruby necklace maybe, or a book of poetry.

Devon sighed, exasperated with himself for still obsessing over Elizabeth. After the way she danced with Todd Wilkins on prom night, he knew there were no ruby necklaces in his future with her. Only friendship.

"You're invited," she'd said near the post office the week before when she invited Devon to the birthday party. He'd felt it then: a twinkle of hope. But Elizabeth had doused the spark by adding, *"I mean, all our friends are."* Clearly he was nothing more than a friend, from Elizabeth's perspective. A single item in the category "all our friends." It felt so cold and impersonal, not at all the way he thought of Elizabeth.

After that encounter he'd chosen her gift with care to convey the same cold, impersonal message she'd sent to him. But now he was having second thoughts about his plan. The present in the box could actually hurt Elizabeth. Did he want to do that to her? *Could* he do it to her?

"No, this is wrong!" Devon muttered under his breath, staring at the wrapped present in his hands as if it were to blame for his problems. Elizabeth had hurt him, but he loved her too much to hurt her intentionally. He would scrap the gift. His backpack lay in the grass beside him. He began to shove the present into it, but suddenly he froze. A tall, well-built boy was stepping out of the house and onto the patio.

Devon's eyes narrowed. "Wilkins!" he said through clenched teeth—though nobody was close enough to hear him even if the band hadn't been playing at top volume.

Todd stood just outside the sliding glass doors, scrutinizing the crowd. When he turned toward the barbecue grill, his posture grew rigid. *He sees Elizabeth,* Devon thought. Sure enough, Todd made a beeline straight for her. He placed a hand on her shoulder, and Elizabeth whirled. And smiled. Penny took one look at them, said something Devon couldn't hear, and slipped away into the crowd. Then Elizabeth and Todd were alone together, standing much closer than Devon thought necessary. And they were completely engrossed in each other—or at least in their conversation.

Devon watched the reunion with a sick sense of dread. "That does it!" he muttered to himself, still sitting in the grass. He couldn't understand how sweet, smart Elizabeth could flirt with Todd in front of Devon and much of the junior class, especially after what she'd done at the prom. "I don't care if I hurt her!" Devon realized.

As soon as he could get her alone, he'd give her the birthday present he'd brought. And Elizabeth would know exactly how bland and low-key their relationship could be.

Todd shifted his weight from one foot to the other. Elizabeth was standing in front of him, as beautiful as ever and apparently happy to see him. Todd had never felt so uncomfortable in her presence.

"Thank you for coming," Elizabeth said. "I didn't think you would."

"I didn't think so either," he admitted. "But I wanted to talk to you."

"Todd, I'm so sorry I hurt you—"

"I know," he interrupted. "We don't have to rehash all that. It won't make any difference."

She nodded slowly. "Then what did you need to tell me?" she said after a moment.

"Liz, I'm going away for the summer. I got a scholarship to a summer basketball camp at the University of North Carolina. I just got the letter today."

"Why North Carolina?" she asked.

Todd shrugged. "UNC at Chapel Hill has one of the best college basketball programs in the country. I can learn a lot there. But there's another reason I chose UNC."

"Because it's far away from here? Far away from me?"

Todd looked away, stuffing his fists into his pockets. "Yeah."

Elizabeth put a hand on his arm, and her touch reminded him of all the good times they'd spent together in the last few years. Most of their time together had been good—no, *perfect*. He'd loved Elizabeth for a long time, and he was afraid he always would. But the good times also brought to mind the arguments and misunderstandings, the nights he'd lain awake wondering what he'd done wrong or whether she still cared about him, and the gut-wrenching sight of Devon Whitelaw's arms around her.

"I'll miss you," Elizabeth said. "I've *been* missing you. But I understand."

Todd's heart felt like it would burst from the strain of being so close to her. "I miss you too, but we both know too much has happened for us to pretend it's all OK."

"You're right."

"Liz, I think it would be best if we didn't write or call each other while I'm back east. I need time apart from you—"

"We both need time apart," Elizabeth interrupted.

Todd nodded. "Yeah, we both need time—a lot of time—to figure out what's left between us and to decide if it's worth salvaging."

"When do you leave?"

"As soon as exams are over."

Elizabeth smiled sadly. "I think it's a good idea for you to get away. You're handling this in a really mature way." She stood on her toes and kissed him on the cheek. "Can we talk in August?"

"Absolutely," he said, kissing her on the forehead. There were tears in her eyes, and moisture was blurring his own vision as well. "Good-bye, Elizabeth."

"Good-bye, Todd."

Todd turned and walked through the crowd, barely noticing the people he was passing by. At the door to the house he stopped to take one last look at Elizabeth, who was using tongs to lift chicken legs from the grill onto a platter Enid was holding. Elizabeth's blouse was kind of a hot pink color, and it glowed under the artificial lights. Her hair shone like gold. Todd stood there for a minute, memorizing the sight of her.

"Happy birthday, Elizabeth," he said in a low voice as a hollow ache filled his heart. An important part of his life was over. But for the first time in weeks he felt a rising excitement about what was to come next. Now that things were resolved—for now—with Elizabeth, the pain and confusion he'd been slogging through seemed to dissolve harmlessly into the dark, heavy, music-filled night. He felt strangely free. And, he realized suddenly, he felt ready to party with his friends.

"Yo, Todd!" called a voice behind him. Todd turned to see Ken Matthews standing in the kitchen. Behind him Olivia was standing near the basement door, which she held slightly ajar. She was speaking in a soothing voice to Prince Albert, who howled and scrabbled against the other side of the door as if he wanted to join the party.

"Hey, Ken," Todd said, reaching out to slap his friend's shoulder. "Sorry again about, uh, interrupting you two out front earlier."

"No big deal, man," Ken said. "Did you talk to Liz?"

Todd nodded. "We agreed to take the summer off from each other. But we're OK."

"You planning to stick around the party for a while?"

"You bet," Todd said. "It's my last chance to see everyone for two months. Besides, I'm starved!"

"Then let's get some snacks," Ken said. "I never realized what an appetite you can work up, making up with a girl."

"You said it!" Todd replied, sliding the door shut behind him. The Droids' music snapped off as the door closed, and for the first time he realized how quiet things were inside the house—if you ignored Prince Albert's sporadic barking. Jazz music had been playing in the living room when Todd arrived, but it seemed to have ended. "I wish I'd snagged one of those chicken legs when I was out at the grill with Liz," he continued. "But I'm not sure I want to go back out there—" He glanced back out the sliding glass door toward Elizabeth.

"No problem," Ken said. "There's plenty of food here in the kitchen. Let's see what we can rustle up."

"You start foraging." Todd grimaced. "I'm dying to use the bathroom. I'll join you back here in a second."

"Are you all right, Liz?" Enid asked in a concerned voice as Elizabeth loaded the last barbecued chicken leg onto the platter.

Elizabeth nodded. "I'm fine. Really."

"Was that what it looked like with Todd?"

She took a deep breath. "That was good-bye. It's all right, Enid. I'm glad Todd and I finally came to some sort of resolution, at least for now. And I'm glad he's going away for the summer. It's what we both need."

"I sense a 'but' coming," Enid said.

"But I'm sad too," Elizabeth admitted. "There was something unnerving about saying good-bye. Something so . . . final."

"It doesn't have to be final," Enid said. "Maybe after a summer apart, you'll realize you really do want to be together."

"Maybe," Elizabeth said. "It's hard to know anything right now. I feel like I've been on a roller-coaster ride. I can't get a handle on my emotions."

"Of course you can't. You and Todd have been together for so long. Give yourself time," Enid advised. "Isn't that why Todd's leaving for the summer?"

"I guess you're right."

"Oh, I almost forgot. Maria Santelli said to tell you the jazz quartet finished up and went home. We scheduled them to leave early, figuring everyone would want to get rowdy with the Droids as the night went on."

As if in response to her comment, the Droids

finished their song and the noise level dipped temporarily. From the far side of the patio Winston who was standing with Maria and Annie, filled the musical void with loud clucking noises.

"I think someone is trying to give me a subtle reminder of my duties as chicken server," Enid called out, holding the platter high. Then she leaned in close to Elizabeth and dropped her voice. "You'll do fine without him, Liz. And you'll have the summer free to think things through. We'll talk later, all right?"

Lila inspected herself in the bathroom mirror. She'd been flirting with Roger Barrett Patman when Jessica—showing her usual lousy timing—had called her to move the Triumph so she and Steven could take the Jeep out of the driveway. Lila hadn't been able to find Roger again when she returned to the party, so she figured it was as good a time as any to retouch her makeup. She pulled a tube of Watermelon Ice lipstick from her Gucci shoulder bag and began to apply it painstakingly.

Somebody banged on the door and Lila jumped. A smear of Watermelon Ice jutted past the outline of her lips. "What's your damage?" she yelled.

"Fowler?" called Todd's voice. "I should have

known it was you. I've been waiting out here forever."

Lila shrugged. "First come, first served, Wilkins. You'll just have to wait your turn."

"Come on, Lila. It doesn't take that long to pee. What could you be doing in there for so long?"

She twisted the corner of a tissue and moistened it under the faucet, then dabbed at the errant smear of lipstick. "You men are so clueless," she complained with a sigh. "What do you think I'm doing? I'm fixing my hair and makeup—"

"I didn't know they were broken," Todd put in.

Lila continued as if he hadn't interrupted. "Not that it's any of your business."

"All I need is two minutes," he said, urgency growing in his voice. "Please!"

Lila smiled wickedly. "I love it when you squirm. Funny, I thought the other jocks were talking about basketball when they gave you the nickname Whizzer Wilkins."

"Lila!"

"You can't actually believe that your bladder is more important than my makeup," she said, rooting through her bag for a mascara. "If you're so desperate, why don't you run upstairs and use the twins' bathroom?"

"I don't have time to run upstairs. I need to go now!"

"You're a big man. You can wait." She found her navy blue mascara and expertly brushed it over her lashes.

"That's it!" Todd yelled. "I don't have to stand for this!" He flung open the door and stood glaring at her. "Now get out of the damn bathroom!"

Lila gasped, dropping her mascara wand. A feathery, navy blue streak scudded across the porcelain sink. "How dare you walk in here like that! I could have poked my eye out. I've never heard of anything so rude—"

"Not as rude as monopolizing the bathroom so you can paint your face when there are people who need it for more important things!"

"You have no right to barge in here like that!" Lila declared, her hands on her hips. "I was here first, and I'm not leaving."

"Oh, yeah?" Todd yelled back. *He'd be more intimidating*, Lila thought, *if he could stop shifting his weight from one foot to the other.*

"If you want me out of here," Lila said, "you'll have to move me by force!" She reached into the sink, scooped out the mascara applicator, and thrust it in front of her like a weapon.

"Maybe I'll just do that!" Todd yelled.

Lila narrowed her eyes at him. "I'd just like to see you try."

Elizabeth arranged some more chicken on the grill and brushed it with some of Steven's secret-recipe barbecue sauce. The Droids hadn't resumed playing yet, and despite dozens of talking and laughing teenagers the yard felt strangely quiet without Dana's amplified alto. From inside the kitchen she could hear Prince Albert's muffled barking, like a warning.

She jumped when somebody close by said her name.

"Oh! Devon!" she cried. "I didn't see you walk up."

"I just wanted to wish you a happy birthday," he said in a surprisingly formal tone.

"Is something wrong? You sound a little weird."

He shook his head and grinned at her, but his eyes looked sad and cold. "No weirder than usual." He held out a wrapped package. "I wanted to give you this. It's a birthday gift that should show you exactly how I feel about you."

Something in his manner made her feel vaguely disturbed, but Elizabeth accepted the gift, which from its size and weight seemed to be a book. As she took it from him her finger lightly touched his. He jerked away.

"Open it now," he urged in a serious voice.

Elizabeth nodded and unwrapped the book. "Thanks, Dev—," she began as she pulled it from the wrapping paper. She stopped when she saw the title. *"Techniques of Journalism,"* she read aloud, a dozen conflicting thoughts racing through her mind.

It was the kind of gift she'd expect from a teacher or a distant relative she'd never met. Thoughtful, she supposed, but not the least bit personal. A gift from a friend, and not even a close friend. *It's the thought that counts,* she scolded herself, feeling guilty for being ungrateful. She set her face into a smile, but then she looked up at Devon's cold smirk. Realization rose within her, and with it anger. If it was the thought that counted, she told herself, then Devon had been thinking vindictive ones when he chose her gift.

"This is supposed to show me exactly how you feel about me?" she asked. "What an obnoxious thing to say!"

"What? You don't like the book?"

"What message am I supposed to be getting from this?" she asked, shaking the book in his face as all the jumbled emotions of the day erupted inside her. "You intentionally chose a boring present so you could prove that you think I'm a boring person?"

Devon folded his arms across his broad chest. "No, not exactly. I—"

"But you don't deny that you picked this out because you wanted to send me a message, and not a very nice one!"

He glared down at her. "No, I don't deny it. And what's more, you deserve it! The way you—"

"Deserve it?" Elizabeth yelled. "I thought we were past the prom. I thought you cared about me as a friend!"

Elizabeth stopped, realizing that every other conversation in the backyard had ceased. But she was still fuming. The Droids immediately launched into a hard-driving rock anthem to fill the silence. For a moment she and Devon glared at each other wordlessly.

"Hi, Liz. Hi, Devon." Maria Santelli's voice broke the stalemate between Devon and Elizabeth. Elizabeth looked up to see Maria and Annie standing beside her, their eyes wide with concern. No doubt, she thought, they were worried about Devon's legendary temper.

"Are you OK, Liz?" Annie asked above the loud rock song.

"I'm fine," she replied.

"Why don't you come into the kitchen with us?" Maria asked. "We should check to make sure there's enough, uh, *ice.*"

"Thanks, but you don't have to rescue me from this conversation," Elizabeth told them, her eyes on Devon's face.

"Get out of here and leave us alone!" Devon snapped at Elizabeth's friends.

Maria's hands flew to her hips, and she stared at him, her mouth open.

"It's OK, Maria," Elizabeth said. "Really."

Annie pulled Maria away. "We'll be in the kitchen," Annie called back over her shoulder as they walked toward the sliding glass doors.

"Yell if you need us," Maria added, casting Devon a hostile glare.

Elizabeth whirled on him as soon as they were gone. "How dare you treat my friends so rudely?" she screamed.

"They'll get over it."

"I can't believe this is happening. A few hours ago I thought that Todd hated me, but you and I were friends. Now Todd and I are OK, but you're acting like I've insulted you somehow!"

"Well, duh!"

"Now there's a shining example of that phenomenal IQ you claim to have—"

"What's that supposed to mean?" he shouted.

Elizabeth shook her head. "It's not supposed to mean anything. You're the one who insulted me!

I'm sorry if I bore you to death, but giving me that book—and saying what you said about it—was a rotten thing to do!"

"It's not about being boring!" Devon screamed. "That's not what I meant! If you weren't always jumping to conclusions—"

"Jumping to conclusions?" she yelled, feeling her face flush with anger. "You're the one who said a cold, impersonal gift would show how you feel about me! Maybe you don't think I'm boring. Maybe you just despise me—"

"I don't despise you! I—"

"Maybe you just despise me," Elizabeth repeated, speaking over his interruption, "but you were too much of a coward to come right out and say it!"

Devon's slate blue eyes darkened. "If you'd give me a chance to explain what I meant—"

"This is about Todd, isn't it?" Elizabeth interrupted. "You said you'd forgiven me, but you haven't! You hate me because you're still mad about the prom!"

"Stop telling me what I'm mad about, and stop telling me how I feel!" Devon shouted.

"And you stop ordering me around!" Elizabeth countered.

"Dammit, Liz, you always think you know everything about everyone!"

"I didn't say—"

"You think you've got everyone's darkest secrets figured out while you're Little Miss Perfect. Well, you have no right to be so sanctimonious! You're the one who was cheating on me!"

Elizabeth felt the color drain from her face. A tiny part of her brain, the part that was still rational, was shocked to realize she actually wanted to strike him. That she was actually going to strike him. She raised a hand to slap him across his strong, angular jaw. . . .

But something hit her first. It slammed into her feet from below, throwing her off balance and jamming every joint in her body. Devon grabbed her arm, the anger in his face transformed to fear. Impossibly, the water in the pool reached up as a single entity, like a sea serpent coming to life, before sloshing back into its container, roiling frenetically. The patio around the pool rippled like water. Deep below the earth's surface a power like nothing Elizabeth had ever imagined rumbled and roared and threatened to tear her world apart. The music went dead.

Then a girl's voice screamed, "Earthquake!"

Chapter 15

Jessica stopped the new Jeep at a red light and turned to stare at her brother. "Gee, thanks a lot, Steven. I assumed Billie was at Edwards' Supermarket, two miles away. It would have been nice of you to tell me we'd have to go clear over to the other side of town."

Steven shrugged. "What's the big deal?" he asked. "It's not like it's that huge a town."

"Why did Billie go all the way to Drakes' convenience store anyway?"

"She said on the phone that Edwards' was out of ice. What difference does it make? It's only a few miles farther. I thought you'd appreciate the chance to drive your new Jeep."

"I get it. You're doing me a favor." The light turned green, and Jessica pressed hard on the accelerator. If she was stuck spending part of her birthday party driving her brother around town, she might as well have some fun along the way.

Steven grabbed the dashboard with both hands to brace himself. "Uh, Jessica, I'd really like to arrive there in one piece. You see, there's this radical new concept known as a speed limit—"

"Lighten up, big brother," Jessica urged.

"Humor me, Jess," Steven begged. "I would really feel better if you slowed down."

"You're still a teenager, remember?" Jessica countered. "You've got a few good years before you have to start acting like a grandpa."

"Not if you keep driving this way!"

Suddenly the Jeep bucked as if something had banged into it from underneath. It swerved to the right. Jessica struggled with the wheel as the vehicle bounced and jerked out of control.

"What the heck are you doing?" Steven screamed. "What did you hit?"

"I didn't hit anything!" Jessica cried, swerving out of the path of a city bus and leaning on her horn. "Yet."

"Then what's happening?"

"My new Jeep is possessed—" Jessica stopped, realizing that outside her window the cars, buildings, and even the street were moving. Suddenly she was aware of a deep roar, like powerful sustained thunder. "Oh, God, Steven. It's an earthquake!"

In the next lane a minivan spun out of control just ahead. Tires squealed, and a station wagon slammed into its bumper with a sickening screech of metal. Jessica briefly considered stopping to see if anyone was hurt, but it was all she could do to keep control of the Jeep, which was jogging up and down as if all four tires were flat.

When the bumping stopped abruptly, Jessica breathed a long sigh. "Thank goodness it's over—," she began.

Steven grabbed her arm. The road ahead had buckled and cracked, throwing up jagged chunks of concrete. Jessica jerked the steering wheel to the left. Just then a powerful aftershock rippled beneath the tires, like a tablecloth being yanked out from under the roadway. The ground lurched. And the Jeep shot over the yellow line and across two lanes of traffic.

Jessica opened her mouth to scream, but no sound came out. A telephone pole loomed directly ahead. Steven's fingers dug painfully into her arm. She slammed on the brakes, but it was too late to stop the Jeep's headlong rush. There was no time to turn. Steven screamed her name. And Jessica briefly wondered if her seventeenth birthday would be her last.

The grassy earth beneath Enid wobbled like gelatin, and she suddenly found herself hurtling to the ground. She shrieked as her entire weight slammed down on one ankle. Pain shot through her leg. This was a hundred—no, a *million*—times worse than the minor earthquake that had struck earlier that day.

Around her in the backyard people screamed or cried out in panic. Somewhere in the distance Prince Albert was barking. But the cries of living creatures were pitifully weak against the cacophony of splitting wood, shattering glass, and creaking metal that filled the night. Beneath it all was the terrifying thunder of earth and stone.

The lights flickered but flashed back on, to Enid's relief. She grasped her ankle and tried to make sense of what was going on around her as the earth continued to tremble. Everything was happening all at once, a collage of nightmare images. . . .

Blood poured from Jade's arm. Aaron's face was streaked with dirt as he clung to the ground. The makeshift wooden stage splintered into fragments as heavy amplifiers and other equipment crashed through the boards. Max Dellon catapulted off the edge and collided with the patio. Penny stumbled toward his still form, sobbing, and leaned over him. . . .

The Wakefield house vibrated against the night sky. Shingles flew off the roof in all directions. Enid screamed and covered her head with her arms. Every joint in her body wrenched with pain as the earth continued to shake.

Enid heard a shout and turned to see Maria Slater fall to the grass near a sturdy old lemon tree. With a sickening roar the tree tore away from the earth, uprooted as easily as a dandelion, and slammed to the ground, covering her friend under a spread of branches. Enid started to crawl toward Maria, but she couldn't even see straight with all the flying debris and the chaos that surrounded her.

Suddenly everything was still. The earthquake was over. Enid realized she'd been holding her breath. She let it out in a long, ragged sigh. But then the earth was shaking again in an aftershock as powerful as the original quake. "No!" she heard herself shrieking.

A terrifying *boom* exploded the night as the chimney ripped off the house and plunged through the roof of the garage. Chunks of building materials and other debris flipped into the pitch-black sky, raining down on the people in the backyard. As Enid watched, a sheet of aluminum siding skidded through the air like a Frisbee. Terrified, Enid flattened herself against the ground.

"Please stop!" she wailed. "Please, please, please . . ."

The kitchen swayed, and Maria Santelli dropped the tumbler she'd been filling with water from the sink. The glass shattered against the Spanish-tiled floor while Maria toppled to her hands and knees, thudding her head against the counter as she fell. Crumbs of glass pierced her skin with small stabs of pain.

On the floor Maria stared around her, dizzy and uncomprehending, as a chorus of screams rose from the backyard. Her eyes focused on one ceramic tile between her hands. The tile was shivering. A fracture appeared at one edge and shot across the colorful ceramic with an audible *crack*. For a moment Maria wondered how a falling glass of water could smash a ceramic tile. Somewhere nearby a dog was barking.

"It's an earthquake!" yelled Olivia, invisible on the far side of the trembling center island. Her voice swept through Maria's mind, clearing the haziness, and the rest of the world shifted into focus. The ceiling was raining pellets and shards of plaster. Maria cowered on the floor, feeling it jerk beneath her as she shielded her head with her arms. Ken must be over near Olivia, she realized, but she couldn't see him either. But Annie had been in the kitchen too. Where was she now?

Prince Albert's barking rose to a higher, more frantic pitch, and Maria searched around her until she spotted the golden retriever under the sturdy butcher-block table. Annie crouched under the table as well, an arm wrapped around the dog's neck. Blood was dripping from Annie's nose.

"Get under the table!" she screamed in Olivia and Ken's direction. "It's safer down here!" There was no answer, but Maria scurried across the buckling floor and slid under the table beside Annie. A thick shower of plaster fragments poured into the room, creating an acrid gray dust that made Maria choke and cough.

"Olivia! Ken!" Annie shouted. "Under here!"

Hugging Annie tightly, Maria peered out from beneath the table. She still couldn't see either of their friends. Somebody was praying out loud. Maria wondered who it was. A few seconds later she realized that the words were coming from her own lips.

⚜ ⚜ ⚜

Todd lurched against Lila as the earth began to rock, and they fell together into the bathtub.

Lila turned on him as indignantly as anyone could, he thought—considering that she was sprawled underneath him. "Todd Wilkins, what do you think you're—" She stopped, and the color drained from her face. The bathtub was trembling beneath them. "Oh, no," she whispered, her breath fluttering hot against his face.

The medicine cabinet flew open with a crash. Its mirrored door shattered as it banged against the wall. Hairbrushes, bottles, and shards of glass leaped from the cabinet and rained down on them. Lila screamed as Todd shielded her face with his arms.

They both cringed as something thudded against the door, slamming it shut. The sound echoed around them, punctuated by rumblings and crashes from farther off.

Todd hugged Lila's trembling form, but it was Elizabeth's face he saw. She was outside. He shoved away images of her body crushed beneath cinder blocks or tossed like a child's toy against the flagstone patio. It was safer to be outside during an earthquake, Todd reminded himself, clutching onto that fact and repeating it firmly under his breath. He wished desperately that he could see Elizabeth right now, to hold her in his arms and know for sure that she was safe.

Olivia heard voices. Maria and Annie were calling her name. So was Ken. She heard their voices over the din of cascading plasterboard and cracking tile, over the dog's yelping, over the distant cries of their friends outside. The lights flickered, sending eerie shadows dancing over the room like black flames. Panting with terror, Olivia leaned against the refrigerator door. Ken had been knocked to the floor. He was scrambling toward her, but the tile rolled like waves, pitching him off balance.

The refrigerator door was smooth and cool against Olivia's back—a welcome contrast to the jumble of textures and rough edges that whirled around her as if caught in a funnel cloud. Her limbs felt heavy, immobile, as if her body were held to the door by magnets.

"Under here!" Maria's scream penetrated the ocean of noises around her, and Olivia knew she had to force her body to move. Through the dust she saw Maria and Annie with Prince Albert, peering out from beneath the kitchen table, their eyes dark and scared. The oak table was large and sturdy. She'd be safe there, she told herself. But it seemed so terribly far away, as if she were looking at the kitchen through the wrong end of a telescope.

"I just have to reach Ken!" she told herself aloud, tearfully. She knew she'd feel a lot braver with his strong arms around her. Together they could make it to the table. Abruptly the room was still. Olivia stared around her, not understanding what was happening.

"Olivia!" Ken yelled, holding a hand out toward her as he struggled to his feet amid a shifting pile of rubble. "Hurry up while the shaking's stopped!"

Olivia was panic-stricken at the thought of leaving the reassuring solidity of the refrigerator, but she knew she had to move, and now. Aftershocks could hit at any minute. Her eyes on Ken's face, she took a deep breath and crawled as quickly as she could over the rubble that covered the broken tile floor. If she could only get to Ken, she told herself irrationally, she would be safe. But her legs moved in slow motion, as in a dream—the most terrifying nightmare of her life.

The silence erupted into another spasm of movement. Ken swore, his terrified gaze fixed on Olivia's halting movements. He waded toward her through piles of rubble. Then a corner of the room gave way, crumbling like papier-mâché. Windows splintered. Water spurted from a hidden pipe. At the same time a resounding crash from the direction of the garage rattled the entire house. He saw Olivia look up, her eyes terrified. A fracture appeared at the break in the plasterboard and rippled across the ceiling like a shot. As Ken watched, Olivia froze.

"Over here! Hurry!" Ken hollered to her, ignoring the acrid smoke that seared his throat.

A slab of plasterboard tore from the ceiling and plunged toward Olivia. It slammed against her upraised arms. Ken screamed. Somewhere behind him Maria cried out tearfully. He shoved aside part of a window frame, desperate to reach Olivia, who was struggling with her bloodstained arms to free herself. Then a giant wooden beam crashed down on top of her.

The house lurched into darkness, as if someone had blown out the lights like a candle. "Olivia!" Ken called again. There was no reply.

Chapter 16

The roof of the house hurled shingles like buckshot, and Devon wove to keep his balance as debris rained down around him. A moment earlier he'd had hold of Elizabeth's arm, but now he spotted her a few feet away. He wondered when she'd been torn away from him. She was treading air as if it were water while dodging glittering coals that spouted from the barbecue grill. He took a faltering step toward Elizabeth. The ground lurched wildly. And with a roar like a cannon, the chimney of the house was uprooted like a tree and cast through the roof of the garage. Devon's mouth dropped open in horror. Suddenly he felt Elizabeth's hand on his shoulder, reassuring. She yelled something into his ear. He couldn't make out the words, but her voice sounded encouraging. Then she pulled him to the ground and crouched beside him to ride out the quake together.

The flagstone patio beneath her was wet and trembling, and Elizabeth had the hideous sensation that she was lying facedown on the back of some enormous, panting sea creature. She wondered where her parents were. And her brother and sister. Steven and Jessica had gone to pick up Billie, and Elizabeth had no idea if they'd returned. She choked back a sob.

"I can't do anything about that now," she whispered to herself. She had to focus on the people she *could* help, if the shaking ever stopped.

Her arm was stretched over Devon's shoulders. His eyes were closed. Tears ran down his face. Elizabeth yelled his name, and his eyelids fluttered open. There was sheer terror in his eyes.

"It's going to be OK!" Elizabeth yelled, more frightened by his petrified expression than by the earthquake itself. Where was calm, clearheaded Devon? She didn't think she could handle this alone.

Frantic shrieks split the night, coming from the house. A deafening surge of crashing and splintering engulfed the voices, and Elizabeth looked up in time to see the roof of her home implode as if it were as weak as a canvas tent.

The earthquake stopped abruptly. The backyard was plunged into darkness—alleviated only by the light of some weak flames that burned in the rubble of the house and the twinkling of a few miniature tin lanterns, the sparks of light from their votive candles reflected, trembling, in the surface of the swimming pool.

Olivia expected to feel pain, but there was none. Debris pummeled her body as a tremendous ripping, splitting, crashing, and thundering rushed over her and around her and seemed to splinter through her entire being. With utter clarity she knew the house was caving in on itself, that it would crush her under its ruins. She pictured Ken's face, with its strong chin and deep-set eyes. He had been trying to reach her when the ceiling fell in. She didn't care about anything else as long as Ken was safe. But she didn't know where he was.

A dreamy sense of quiet filled Olivia; the clamor receded. The only sound she could hear clearly was the howling of a dog. Wood, metal, and masonry still showered over her, burying her. Through a momentary chink in the rubble above she caught a glimpse, the faint glimmer of a distant star. And she slipped calmly into darkness.

*　　*　　*

Winston lurched to his feet in darkness as soon as the earth stopped rocking. He wrapped his arms around himself, wondering why he felt so cold. There was a ringing in his ears, mixed up with the crunch of debris settling into the rubble of the destroyed home. He doubted anyone could have survived if they'd been inside as the building collapsed. But he was pretty sure the house had been empty. He remembered Maria saying the jazz quartet had gone home, leaving the party guests to gravitate to the backyard.

Maria. Where was she? Why couldn't he think?

A violent aftershock blasted him to his hands and knees, and he clung to the lawn. He peered around him wildly, trying to discern anything or anyone in the black night. The air smelled of chlorine, natural gas, and the acrid smoke of electrical fires—blended, surreally, with the aroma of barbecued chicken.

He had to find Maria. He'd last seen her in the kitchen, he remembered suddenly, his stomach clenching. But she'd promised to come back outside soon. Surely she'd been on the patio when the earthquake struck. She had to have been.

Because no one could have survived inside the rubble that was once the Wakefield home.

❖   ❖   ❖

Somewhere a girl was screaming. Enid lifted her head cautiously, the earth still bucking beneath her. She heard Prince Albert's yelps too, but she couldn't see the dog. The girl's screams grew louder, more urgent, and Enid half rose from the patio to see if she could help. Pain sliced through her ankle, and she sank back to the wet pavement.

Suddenly a hideous torrent of sound roared over the urgent cries of the unseen girl and the frantic dog. Enid held her breath, helpless. And the Wakefield home deflated, crumbling inward like a falling soufflé. At the same moment the earth rolled to an uneasy halt. Every electric light blinked out.

Enid squinted to make out her surroundings by the remaining pinpricks of light on the patio. She was a few feet from the pool, near the house. For a moment it seemed that everything was still. Then another crash erupted from the house and a section of the roof thundered toward the patio.

"Look out!" someone yelled.

Enid glanced around wildly, looking for somewhere safe to move to. She thought she caught a glimpse of Elizabeth. Then something heavy slammed into the side of Enid's head, and the crushing pain obliterated everything else.

❖ ❖ ❖

228

A figure raced out of the darkness toward Winston. It was Cheryl Thomas. He clutched her arms and struggled to speak. Maybe she'd seen Maria. But his tongue wouldn't form the words.

"Winston, have you seen Annie?" Cheryl asked, her voice raw. Tension radiated off her body. Winston shook his head. Cheryl's father had married Annie Whitman's mother just a few months earlier, and the combined family had moved into the house next door to the Wakefields'. It was too dark to tell if the house was intact now.

"What is it, Win?" Cheryl asked. "Are you hurt?"

Winston opened his mouth, but he was breathing too heavily to choke out the words.

"Your hands are like ice," Cheryl told him, wriggling out of her oversize jacket. "You may be in shock. Here, take my jacket. We should keep you warm." He didn't protest as she wrapped the jacket around his shoulders.

Cheryl glanced toward the spot where her own house stood—if it still stood. "Maybe I should go home, see if my parents—"

"Winston! Is that you?" called another girl's voice. Sara Eastbourne came running out of the darkness from the direction of the pool. Tears were streaming down her face. "Oh, Cheryl, I'm glad you're here too. Are you two OK?"

"Winston's in shock," Cheryl said.

Finally he found his voice. "Maria!" he choked out. "Has either of you seen Maria Santelli?"

Cheryl's eyes looked stricken. "Oh, God, Winston. I've been so worried about Annie, I wasn't thinking. You must be as frantic as I am."

"You guys, Annie and Maria—" Sara choked on a sob.

"What is it, Sara?" Cheryl demanded. "What about them?"

The fear in Sara's eyes made Winston's stomach contract. "What about Annie and Maria?" he whispered, repeating Cheryl's question. "Tell us!"

Sara took his hand and squeezed it. "They were both in the kitchen before the earthquake struck."

"No!" Winston cried, unwilling to believe that Maria could be lying under a pile of rubble. "That's not true! They told me they were coming back outside in just a minute. They must have made it out in time!"

Sara shook her head. "No, Winston. I was standing outside the sliding glass door when the ground started to move. Annie and Maria were still inside the house. Ken and Olivia too."

Winston was trembling, but this time it was coming from deep inside his own body. He couldn't remember ever feeling so cold. He shook his head helplessly, staring from Sara's face to Cheryl's. Then he wrenched his hand away from Sara's and began to run, staggering, toward the house. Close behind him both of the girls were following, screaming for help.

The aftershock lifted the Jeep off the ground. Jessica gripped the steering wheel of the speeding car, her knuckles a deathly white. When the tires hit the pavement, she pressed both feet against the brake pedal until she felt the floor, braking so hard she was practically standing up. Tires wailed against the roadway, rubber burning with an acrid reek. But the Jeep raced forward, unchecked, like an airplane plummeting to earth.

Steven was screaming. The telephone pole rushed toward them, and Jessica instinctively threw her hands up to protect her face. Her body pitched forward, straining against her seat belt. Metal crumpled around her like paper. For a split second her sister's face flashed before Jessica's eyes, and she wished desperately that she knew for sure whether Elizabeth was safe. Then Jessica's body smashed into the windshield. And everything went black.

Who will live? Who will die? Find out in Sweet Valley High **Earthquake,** *coming soon to a store near you!*

Bantam Books in the Sweet Valley High series
Ask your bookseller for the books you have missed

#1 DOUBLE LOVE	#52 WHITE LIES
#2 SECRETS	#53 SECOND CHANCE
#3 PLAYING WITH FIRE	#54 TWO-BOY WEEKEND
#4 POWER PLAY	#55 PERFECT SHOT
#5 ALL NIGHT LONG	#56 LOST AT SEA
#6 DANGEROUS LOVE	#57 TEACHER CRUSH
#7 DEAR SISTER	#58 BROKENHEARTED
#8 HEARTBREAKER	#59 IN LOVE AGAIN
#9 RACING HEARTS	#60 THAT FATAL NIGHT
#10 WRONG KIND OF GIRL	#61 BOY TROUBLE
#11 TOO GOOD TO BE TRUE	#62 WHO'S WHO?
#12 WHEN LOVE DIES	#63 THE NEW ELIZABETH
#13 KIDNAPPED!	#64 THE GHOST OF TRICIA MARTIN
#14 DECEPTIONS	#65 TROUBLE AT HOME
#15 PROMISES	#66 WHO'S TO BLAME?
#16 RAGS TO RICHES	#67 THE PARENT PLOT
#17 LOVE LETTERS	#68 THE LOVE BET
#18 HEAD OVER HEELS	#69 FRIEND AGAINST FRIEND
#19 SHOWDOWN	#70 MS. QUARTERBACK
#20 CRASH LANDING!	#71 STARRING JESSICA!
#21 RUNAWAY	#72 ROCK STAR'S GIRL
#22 TOO MUCH IN LOVE	#73 REGINA'S LEGACY
#23 SAY GOODBYE	#74 THE PERFECT GIRL
#24 MEMORIES	#75 AMY'S TRUE LOVE
#25 NOWHERE TO RUN	#76 MISS TEEN SWEET VALLEY
#26 HOSTAGE	#77 CHEATING TO WIN
#27 LOVESTRUCK	#78 THE DATING GAME
#28 ALONE IN THE CROWD	#79 THE LONG-LOST BROTHER
#29 BITTER RIVALS	#80 THE GIRL THEY BOTH LOVED
#30 JEALOUS LIES	#81 ROSA'S LIE
#31 TAKING SIDES	#82 KIDNAPPED BY THE CULT!
#32 THE NEW JESSICA	#83 STEVEN'S BRIDE
#33 STARTING OVER	#84 THE STOLEN DIARY
#34 FORBIDDEN LOVE	#85 SOAP STAR
#35 OUT OF CONTROL	#86 JESSICA AGAINST BRUCE
#36 LAST CHANCE	#87 MY BEST FRIEND'S BOYFRIEND
#37 RUMORS	#88 LOVE LETTERS FOR SALE
#38 LEAVING HOME	#89 ELIZABETH BETRAYED
#39 SECRET ADMIRER	#90 DON'T GO HOME WITH JOHN
#40 ON THE EDGE	#91 IN LOVE WITH A PRINCE
#41 OUTCAST	#92 SHE'S NOT WHAT SHE SEEMS
#42 CAUGHT IN THE MIDDLE	#93 STEPSISTERS
#43 HARD CHOICES	#94 ARE WE IN LOVE?
#44 PRETENSES	#95 THE MORNING AFTER
#45 FAMILY SECRETS	#96 THE ARREST
#46 DECISIONS	#97 THE VERDICT
#47 TROUBLEMAKER	#98 THE WEDDING
#48 SLAM BOOK FEVER	#99 BEWARE THE BABY-SITTER
#49 PLAYING FOR KEEPS	#100 THE EVIL TWIN (MAGNA)
#50 OUT OF REACH	
#51 AGAINST THE ODDS	

#101	THE BOYFRIEND WAR	#120	IN LOVE WITH THE ENEMY
#102	ALMOST MARRIED	#121	THE HIGH SCHOOL WAR
#103	OPERATION LOVE MATCH	#122	A KISS BEFORE DYING
#104	LOVE AND DEATH IN LONDON	#123	ELIZABETH'S RIVAL
#105	A DATE WITH A WEREWOLF	#124	MEET ME AT MIDNIGHT
#106	BEWARE THE WOLFMAN (SUPER THRILLER)	#125	CAMP KILLER
#107	JESSICA'S SECRET LOVE	#126	TALL, DARK, AND DEADLY
#108	LEFT AT THE ALTAR	#127	DANCE OF DEATH
#109	DOUBLE-CROSSED	#128	KISS OF A KILLER
#110	DEATH THREAT	#129	COVER GIRLS
#111	A DEADLY CHRISTMAS (SUPER THRILLER)	#130	MODEL FLIRT
#112	JESSICA QUITS THE SQUAD	#131	FASHION VICTIM
#113	THE POM-POM WARS	#132	ONCE UPON A TIME
#114	"V" FOR VICTORY	#133	TO CATCH A THIEF
#115	THE TREASURE OF DEATH VALLEY	#134	HAPPILY EVER AFTER
#116	NIGHTMARE IN DEATH VALLEY	#135	LILA'S NEW FLAME
#117	JESSICA THE GENIUS	#136	TOO HOT TO HANDLE
#118	COLLEGE WEEKEND	#137	FIGHT FIRE WITH FIRE
#119	JESSICA'S OLDER GUY	#138	WHAT JESSICA WANTS . . .
		#139	ELIZABETH IS MINE
		#140	PLEASE FORGIVE ME
		#141	A PICTURE-PERFECT PROM?
		#142	THE BIG NIGHT
		#143	PARTY WEEKEND!

SUPER EDITIONS:
PERFECT SUMMER
SPECIAL CHRISTMAS
SPRING BREAK
MALIBU SUMMER
WINTER CARNIVAL
SPRING FEVER
FALLING FOR LUCAS
JESSICA TAKES MANHATTAN
MYSTERY DATE
LAST WISH
EARTHQUAKE
AFTERSHOCK

SUPER THRILLERS:
DOUBLE JEOPARDY
ON THE RUN
NO PLACE TO HIDE
DEADLY SUMMER
MURDER ON THE LINE
BEWARE THE WOLFMAN
A DEADLY CHRISTMAS
MURDER IN PARADISE
A STRANGER IN THE HOUSE
A KILLER ON BOARD
"R" FOR REVENGE

SUPER STARS:
LILA'S STORY
BRUCE'S STORY
ENID'S STORY
OLIVIA'S STORY
TODD'S STORY

MAGNA EDITIONS:
THE WAKEFIELDS OF
    SWEET VALLEY
THE WAKEFIELD LEGACY:
    THE UNTOLD STORY
A NIGHT TO REMEMBER
THE EVIL TWIN
ELIZABETH'S SECRET DIARY
JESSICA'S SECRET DIARY
RETURN OF THE EVIL TWIN
ELIZABETH'S SECRET DIARY
    VOLUME II
JESSICA'S SECRET DIARY
    VOLUME II
THE FOWLERS OF
    SWEET VALLEY
THE PATMANS OF
    SWEET VALLEY
ELIZABETH'S SECRET DIARY
    VOLUME III
JESSICA'S SECRET DIARY
    VOLUME III